Returning to Ionia

A Story of Love and War

CONSTANTINE SANTAS

iUniverse®

RETURNING TO IONIA
A STORY OF LOVE AND WAR

iUniverse books may be ordered through booksellers or by contacting:

iUniverse
1663 Liberty Drive
Bloomington, IN 47403
www.iuniverse.com
844-349-9409

ISBN: 978-1-6632-1474-4 (sc)
ISBN: 978-1-6632-1473-7 (hc)
ISBN: 978-1-6632-1475-1 (e)

Library of Congress Control Number: 2020924602

Print information available on the last page.

iUniverse rev. date: 12/14/2020

CONTENTS

Part III: The Return

ACKNOWLEDGMENTS

I wish to acknowledge my debt to entrepreneur and philhellene Nick Lazaris for reading large sections of the original manuscript and making suggestions for its improvement; my warm thanks to Dr. Eugenia Charoni, assistant professor of Romance languages at Flagler College, for helping me to convert sections of the manuscript from typewritten text to Microsoft Word; Professor Gerasimos Santas of UCI for critiquing and commenting on large sections of the book; and my late father, Xenophon Santas, for allowing me to tape his memories of World War II, which helped me to design the structure of the story and enrich its contents. And to my son, Aristotle Santas, PhD, for his consistent reading and evaluation of independent short stories incorporated in *Returning to Ionia*. Also, I owe great thanks to Dr. Darien Andrew, English professor at Flagler College, for having read many of my stories of the war and offering me enthusiastic guidelines in creative writing.

ACKNOWLEDGMENTS

AUTHOR'S NOTE

Although largely based on historical events, the occupation of Greece by Italy's Fascist dictatorship of Benito Mussolini, and the Nazis of Adolf Hitler of Germany, this narrative is fictional in its entirety. The narrator, a boy, aged ten to fifteen—through the duration of the war—is entirely invented, as are the characters in the story and the narrated events. I spent many years writing the stories and reading them to audiences on occasion. Some were published in literary magazines while I was still a student and some in blogs today. Most, however, remained unpublished and gradually became what one might call the nexus of the present narrative.

My emphasis was in plotting a narrative of episodes I had written over a long time, and, as I went along, I sought to turn a pastiche of disparate parts into a streaming whole. The narrative relates historical events as they occurred, but a love story runs through it, which adds to the emotional reactions of a coming-of-age youngster. The boy's perspective is ironic, as he guesses and even predicts that the characters and situations with which he is involved make him a judge of human behavior under stress and make his point of view omniscient. This is an essential and, in some ways, daring innovation in narrative, and the reader will decide whether I have succeeded.

One final word about the title: *Returning to Ionia* is mostly a reference to the last part of the story, which tells the reader about the protagonist and his return to the place of his birth and is busy still designing the ending of his story. Ionia is a made-up name, an unidentified place in the western part of Greece, the Ionian Sea, dotted with the famous Seven Islands, conquered by the Venetian Empire, which later became part of the British Empire and were donated to Greece by Queen Victoria, on the occasion of the ascension to the throne of King George I in 1964.

PART I

Bonds of War

CHAPTER 1

October

September came, sluggish and damp. The year was 1940, and war was in the air. I was in the third grade of the Octataxion, an eight-grade high school, as the prime minister, John Metaxas, the dictator of Greece, rearranged the school curriculum to fit his ambitions of a newer and purer Greek nation. Grade school was reduced to only four grades, after which one had to enter the Octataxion by taking a rather frivolous exam. I was only nine then, and the professor at the desk asked me to name a four-legged animal.

"A goat," I said.

"You passed," he responded, and I became a new Octataxion student.

I had to wear a special outfit during parades and other ceremonies. Like other students, I became a member of the National Greek Youth Organization[1] and received its newspaper from Athens on a regular basis. August 4, 1936, was proclaimed a national holiday, as this was the date Metaxas came to power, and we students had to learn to sing a song equivalent to the national anthem: "This day came the light

---

[1] *Ελληνική Ένωσις Νέων.*

of August fourth," the tune went as we marched. I learned to salute the taxiarchs, pompous paramilitary officers who wore expensive uniforms with gold epaulets and were paid double the salary of the regular army officers. The dictator posed as Greece's new savior, and he had the power to crush his opposition and force the common Greeks to bow their heads.

I was too young to realize what all that meant and went along with the crowd. I also came to know, then and later in my schooling, that we Greeks were special because our "glorious ancestors" had given the world the lights of civilization. Teachers, whether affiliated with Metaxas or not, were pounding into our heads the victories of the Greeks over the Persians at Marathon and Salamis, thus saving the world from "barbarism" and saying that Homer was the first and greatest of poets. As history was my favorite subject, I absorbed these lessons eagerly and spent hours on my own, reading stories of the Trojan War, Alexander's conquests, and Odysseus's feats in battling monsters and coming back to Ithaca to slay the suitors. The school edition of *The Odyssey* was my third-grade textbook. (I saved it and kept reading it until one of my aunts, not knowing what it was, used its pages to light the fire.)

I was sailing along and passed the first and second grades of the Octataxion with good grades and started the third grade, facing the new challenge of Latin, which was added to the curriculum. September soon unfolded into October, and some rumblings of the coming war reached my ears. For one thing, my father's brother, Stathis, who lived with us and lectured on civil defense, came home one day, saying that the Italians—he mentioned Benito Mussolini—would soon attack Greece. Airplanes, he said, would drop incendiary bombs, which would start fires or spread poisonous gasses that would choke us to death, unless we wore masks. Stathis added that Mussolini had dropped such gasses in Ethiopia, which had surrendered to Italy and was now part of the Italian Empire.

"But Metaxas wants to join the Axis," my father said one morning at the table.

"He is pro-German," Stathis explained, "but Benito wants to

annex Greece. And he will attack—and soon. And when he takes Greece, Hitler will name Metaxas as his proxy. That's how Benito kills two birds with one stone."

"Let him attack," my father said. "We will fight him and push him back. The Greeks aren't anybody's proxy!"

"And how about our pensions?" asked a neighbor, Photis, who used to join us in our house for his morning coffee. He was an ex–navy officer and wore his frayed uniform and twirled his cane between his knees. "We can't live without our pensions."

"How is Garoufalia?" my father asked him.

"Scared, like you and me." Garoufalia (meaning *carnation*), one of my father's first cousins, was a shy, elderly woman who always stayed home. She was overwhelmed by the local bishop's denouncement of women named after flowers, rather than being given Christian names (another in the neighborhood was called Lemonia, or *lemon tree*). Though the bishop was a benign father figure and meant well, those women took his words as a sign they were going to hell. War had heightened those fears, as all in the neighborhood expected to die in flames or be choked to death by aerial gasses.

"War is war," Stathis said, "and we'll lose more than pensions." He rushed out of the house to make his morning classes. He was our physical education instructor. I snatched my school bag and followed him.

It was now late October. In addition to Latin, I had to take French, so I was tackling two foreign languages, plus the "killer"—Ancient Greek, a course loathed by students for its twisted syntax and the punitive method it was taught. One had to memorize everything—prepositions, noun inflexions, verbs that had two past tenses plus a progressive one, etc. A pompous, round-bellied teacher called Perdakaris usually entered the room and started reciting prepositions before he said good morning. He took great pride in his pedagogic skills, and he demanded that we memorize everything in the grammar textbook. We called his method *parrot talk*, and some of us started reciting propositions and verbs in the schoolyard to get a good grade from him. I shouted out the prepositions one evening in my room to prepare for next day's test, and I was so loud that my mother thought I had a fever. She made me go to bed and brought me tea and gave me an aspirin.

One day I asked my uncle Stathis to explain to me why we were learning ancient Greek, which had not been spoken for more than two thousand years, and we were supposed to be proud of ourselves too. He explained that was the will of Metaxas, who wished to mold modern Greek youths after our famous ancestors. I asked him why grammar would make us better Greeks. He shrugged his shoulders and said that learning a language would be to my advantage and recommended that I hit the books and pass my tests. I didn't like that.

Next morning, I had a class with Manodis, the French professor, who was so entertaining I didn't mind his lessons. He wore a black suit, white shirt, black bowtie, and patent leather shoes, and his shirt sleeves exuded perfume, causing the girls sitting in the first row to swoon as he passed by. He walked as if stepping on a tightrope, making sharp right angles through the room, and held a ferule that he pointed to a student like an archer aiming for a bull's-eye. (Someone whispered to me once that he had aimed to be a ballet dancer but failed.)

Fifteen minutes into his lecture, the sound of the siren shattered the morning quiet. We'd heard this sound before during the civil defense tests, although there had been warnings before those. But this time, the sharp, metallic blare was for real. Before the professor could react, Stathis bolted into the room, yelling, "Downstairs to the shelter!" He had trained us to be orderly, but the rushing from the emptying classroom became chaotic, and the girls screamed as they trotted down the stairs. Even before the basement was filled, we heard the roar of planes, and the sound of explosions shook the ground under our feet. I lay back against the basement wall, lowering my head against my knees and holding my legs tightly with both hands. A boy next to me vomited, and a girl squeezed her cheeks and yelled, her glasses falling to the ground. I closed my eyes and sat there, my heart pounding inside my chest.

Minutes passed—five, ten—then the sound of the siren started again, its long whine indicating the end of the air raid.

Stathis, helped by some of the other instructors, directed the student crowd to the yard, where we filed in class units, still not knowing what the damages were from the horrifying raid just moments ago.

Manodis, still unruffled, stood in a line with other professors. There were thirteen of them, the fourteenth being the principal, Mr. Tsolakis, who climbed on a podium to deliver a speech. He was a balding, middle-aged man, who wiped his heavily perspiring face and cleaned his glasses with his handkerchief. He looked shaky and indecisive.

"He's got shit in his pants," a fellow student next to me said.

"His days are numbered. The next bomb will fall on his head," said another.

Tsolakis was known for his pro-Metaxas views and had urged us in his speeches to revere the August 4 celebrations in the same way we celebrated March 25, the national Greek Independence Day. Sweating and huffing, Tsolakis coughed and started his oration—length: three sentences.

"Mussolini sent Greece an ultimatum to surrender. Prime Minister Metaxas said *no*! School is dismissed until further notice."

"Wow! School's dismissed," I said to myself.

All rushed to the exit as the siren started again. But this time, its whine was long—a signal that the raid was over, this time for good.

"Metaxas said *no*?" Photis asked, as my mother, still shaking from the terror of the raid, served him his coffee.

"What was the damage?" my father asked Stathis.

"Overall, not much," Stathis responded. "One of the bombs fell on the Venetian Fort"—the Venetians themselves had built it—"and the other hit the ferryboat in the canal, killing a few cows and a donkey, but the men on it jumped into the sea. The third bomb exploded on the Salt Works, turning tons of salt back into sea water. Typical of Benito, a buffoon who thinks he is Julius Caesar." He had a penchant for sarcasm, even at the darkest hour. But his remarks provided some comic relief for his audience, who still were shaken by the experience of the raid, just about an hour earlier.

Our dining room downstairs served as the news center in the neighborhood, and my mother, always hospitable, served coffee and cookies to the guests. More arrived in a few minutes, among them Stathis's fiancée, Katia, and his friend Achilles Chufas, our math teacher. The three of them were often seen together, and rumor had it that both men vied for Katia, a beautiful brunette, who also taught at the high school. Garoufalia, living in the neighborhood, had whispered something to my mother one day, and I quickly caught up.

"What do you think, Achilles?" my father asked the math teacher, who was a frequent guest at our house. "Does Metaxas mean it when he said no, or will he allow Benito to run through the country?"

Achilles was a laconic fellow who never offered an opinion in a full sentence. "Don't know … don't know. Maybe," was all he said.

"Let's listen to the radio," said Photis, who had brought one with him. As he turned it on, it was playing the national anthem, and then came an official statement that "our soldiers are fighting on our ancestral land." All concluded that the Italians were advancing.

But both Achilles and Stathis now focused on Katia, whose eyes had swollen with tears that she wiped with her handkerchief.

"What's the matter, dear?" said Stathis. "Why are you crying?"

Instead of answering, she reached into her handbag and pulled out a letter. "Here," she said, still sponging her tears. "I am being transferred to Gytheion!"

"Gytheion!" cried Stathis. "That's five hundred kilometers away!" He grabbed the letter and read it anxiously.

"That's a township near Sparta," said Photis irrelevantly. "You will reside next to a city of ancient glory. She will be safe there. The Spartans will fight. And they were never defeated!"

"That's all hot air!" my father exploded. "Sparta nowadays is a small town. Mussolini's tanks will wipe it from the face of the earth in minutes!"

Hearing that, Katia burst out crying, with sobs so violent that my mother hurried to bring her a glass of water and an aspirin.

Stathis and Achilles helped the young lady get to her feet, and then they hustled her out of the house, and all three left without even saying goodbye or a thank-you to my mother.

"Women always get shook up in moments of crisis," said Photis, whose remarks always fell short of impressing his audience. "How about me and my pension?" He exited after thanking my mother for his morning coffee, and we heard his cane clacking on the stone pavement outside.

"He's such a nuisance," my father said, looking at me. "What are we going to do with him?" he asked my mother. "He'll not be safe here if more bombs fall."

"Send him to my father's in the village," she said. "He used to spend his summer's there."

I was shrunk in a corner, eating a slice of toasted bread.

"Off to your grandfather's in the village you go," my father told me.

"I'll help you get your things," my mother said.

We both went upstairs, where she started placing clothes and other small items in a leather bag. She also asked me to put my schoolbooks there, and I did, adding a novel I had been reading, borrowed from my friend Panos, next door. It was one of Jules Verne's stories, and I was right in the middle of it.

"Stop reading fantasies," my mother advised. "They're no good for you. Concentrate on your schoolbooks."

But after a pleading look from me, she let me have it, and right away, I thought maybe this war might be a nice little vacation from hard work after all.

By midafternoon, a relative from my grandfather's village arrived with his donkey. The animal, tied in the yard for a few minutes, started braying, making a ruckus louder than the siren had that morning. But it didn't protest when I sat on the saddle, with the help of a relative, who was called Vasilis. Half an hour later, we had gained enough ground up the hills to view the town, which was enveloped in an ugly mist.

CHAPTER 2

Money from America

The military truck climbed past the Stavros vineyards, wound up another hill, disappeared behind a bend, and then swerved to the right at the mouth of the plateau, left the highway, and took a side road toward the village. I watched it labor past Grandfather's house, its tires tearing against the cobblestones, slinging mud at any passersby.

"It's picking up recruits at the square," Grandmother said, as she placed her knit shawl over her shoulders. "I'm going there to say goodbye to one of my nephews."

"I'm coming too," Grandfather mumbled, rising from his corner seat, ready to follow her.

"Don't you see it's raining?" she said, stopping him in his tracks. "You'll catch your death out there."

Grandfather sank back in his chair, sighing and looking disheartened. "Why are the bells ringing?" he asked weakly. "What's going on?"

"Must be another city we've taken."

I smelled news, so I asked her to let me go with her, and she said yes. To be sure, as soon as we were out of the gate, a man came up the lane, out of breath.

"I just heard the bulletin on the radio," he announced. "Korytsa was taken."

That was another victory at the front, he said, as the Greek soldiers had pushed back the Italians and had taken the Greek city of Korytsa, inside Albania. The Greeks called that section *Albanian Greece*, as most of its inhabitants were Greeks.

Grandmother forced her umbrella open, providing shelter for both of us, though my shoulder and right elbow were getting wet. I had now spent several weeks at my grandfather's and was used to walking on the cobblestones of the narrow streets without slipping and falling (which had happened several times).

I outdistanced my grandmother and got to the station first, leaving her huffing behind in the falling drizzle.

Some men had come out of the village coffeehouse and formed a group, chatting about the news.

"We're kicking their butts," one of the men was saying. "The evzones[2] are doing it too. Mussolini has tanks. Greeks have hearts."

"Korytsa is a Greek town," another man remarked, though it was in Albania. "Northern Epirus is ours. The English know that; they'll let us keep it after the war."

"Don't count on the English giving anything to you," cracked a third man. "They're not used to giving, just taking."

"They are our allies," another man countered. "Don't bad-mouth them."

"You morons. We're a small country, and they're kicking us around like a soccer ball. Don't expect mercy from any of the mighty."

"Did the midwife twist your belly button when you were born?" added a tall, white-haired shepherd, with his staff resting horizontally on his shoulders. "Aren't we beating this macaroni-eater? I fought in the First World War, and we turned our enemies' rears into shitholes. Quit that crap, and go home and join your wives, who are knitting socks for the men in the front." He spat on the ground and walked away.

---

[2] Kilted soldiers, a special unit of Greek fighting forces.

"He's a Vlach from Acarnania. What do you expect?" one of the men said. "Because they have cattle and corn, they think they own us."

I left the group still wrangling among themselves—my father had said Greeks never agreed on anything—and joined my grandmother, who just had arrived on the scene, still huffing from the effort of climbing (she was a large woman). She had gone near the recruits who were lining up behind the truck, waiting for their names to be called. An officer counted them, wet his pencil with his lips, and scribbled something on a pad. When a name was called out, each man was separated from his relatives, mostly old folks; climbed up the back of the truck; and sat on a bench under a thick canvas. This scene lasted about thirty minutes in a steadily falling drizzle.

When Grandmother's nephew, Nicholas, was called, she hugged him hastily, before he drew away. Nicholas, tall and ruggedly handsome, his hair waving back, said nothing.

"That hair will be shaved to the skin," a fellow behind him joked.

"Don't care about the hair," Nicholas responded. "Shaved head and all, I will kill Italians."

"When we catch him, we will shave Benito's hair," another man remarked, and they all laughed, enjoying his joke.

Nicholas's mother, a woman in black, clung to him.

"All right, lady," the officer said to her, sticking his pencil behind his ear. "We'll get him back to you in no time."

She let him go, and he sat on the bench, smiling stiffly. Soon, the truck rolled down the muddy cobblestones and disappeared behind some trees.

When we got back to the house, Grandfather had stepped out onto his balcony.

"Christo!" Grandmother cried, ready to scold him.

"I couldn't see a thing when they passed by," he complained. "They put them under that canvas. Damn!" He looked sullen and cold as a fish.

Grandmother gently pulled him by the arm and led him into the kitchen, where a fire was blazing. She helped him sit on his stool and gave him herbal tea and a sweet roll. Then she made sure the cape was over his shoulders.

"Don't be upset, Christo," she reassured him. "Metaxas is a good man. He won't let the Fascists kill our young people. Besides, think of Constantine, who will have to give up his truck. The poor fellow has five mouths to feed. What'll become of him?"

"What will become of us?"

"We have our fields. We won't go hungry."

"What if the Italians get us?"

"They won't get us," Grandmother said, stamping her foot. "Haven't you heard? We're taking their towns!"

The old man kept mumbling words to himself, sniffling furiously. But he let Grandmother coddle him, as she usually did. He slurped his tea, munched his sweet roll, and fell silent. A few minutes later, I heard him snore.

Next morning, my father arrived to see how I was doing and to bring provisions—small sacks filled with sugar and coffee, as well as some dried cod fish for Grandfather, who was diabetic and did not relish meat. Though we heard the sirens blowing every morning, there had been no other air raids in town, only across the bay at Preveza, where the Italians dropped their bombs regularly every morning about eleven on the military depots there—the depots stored supplies for the front lines.

"People are getting used to the sirens," Father said. He had enlarged the shelter inside the wall in the basement, and they were crouching in there when they heard the planes. He said schools were about to reopen soon, a piece of information not entirely to my taste.

I asked him to let me stay a few days longer, and he only said that my mother missed me.

Father took the rest of the day to build a bomb shelter in Grandfather's backyard—in case any stray bombs were dropped on the village. He also said the falling anti-aircraft shells had dug holes on the nearby hills, and anyone could be injured during raids.

Grandfather readily gave his consent, listening as my father explained the dangers of air raids over coffee in the kitchen.

They sent for Vasilis, who lived in the neighborhood, to help. Since the day he brought me to the village, Vasilis and I had become friends. Vasilis was cross-eyed, and some people called him slow-witted. But he was a hard worker, and pretty soon, a hole, as big as a grave, was gaping in the back lot under an almond tree. When it was about six feet deep, my father laid heavy planks over it, while Vasilis carried large bags filled with dirt to place over the planks. This part of the job took a long time, and it didn't seem they would finish the shelter that afternoon.

Grandfather came out of the house several times to check on the progress of the work and nodded his head approvingly. He turned to me. "Go to Kosmas's and tell your uncle George he's needed here. Tell him to hurry."

Uncle George was Grandfather's only son who had not immigrated to America, and he was supervising all the fieldwork on Grandfather's property.

I trotted off, eager to be of use. After all, I was staying at the old man's house, doing nothing all day but reading books and roaming about his yard, so I might as well be of help.

As I turned up the lane, I spotted my cousin Eleni, a pretty girl who was my schoolmate, driving home two goats from pasture. She blushed as she went by, not saying a word, although I knew she had recognized me; she probably was embarrassed that I had caught her doing the chores of a shepherdess. I hadn't seen her since the war had started, a few weeks back. She was my friend Panos's sweetheart—I knew that for a fact—although, of course, I had eyes for her too. That was my secret.

I turned into a side lane, and soon I was at Kosmas's. The smell of crushed kernels was so pungent that it caught my breath as I stepped inside. The place was steamy, like a hothouse, the refuse on the floor evaporating oily humidity and keeping the temperature comfortable.

Grandfather was right. Uncle George was lounging on one of the kernel piles, idly gazing at the horses in the treadmill, joking and talking with the other fellows in there. Those were village teens, just below draft age, who worked alongside two or three middle-aged men. George, at thirty-eight, had not been drafted.

"Grandfather wants you at home, Uncle," I said, aware that all eyes focused on me.

"Look at his short pants," one of the youths said. "Doesn't he catch cold?"

"And at his weird haircut," said another, alluding to my obligatory school crew cut, now grown two inches. They all cracked up.

"Tell him I'll be home by and by," Uncle George said, evidently unbothered that his coworkers had made jokes at his nephew's expense.

"All right, I will," I responded gloomily and ran out.

When I got back to Grandfather's, the mailman had just arrived from town and had delivered a big envelope.

"It's a letter from your uncles in America," Grandmother explained to me.

Grandfather was holding the opened envelope in his hands, out of which he had taken a check with large print on it. Both he and my father sat in front of the fire in the kitchen, sipping herbal tea.

"How much is it?" Grandfather asked, handing my father the check.

"Four thousand dollars."

"And how much Greek money is that?"

"Seventy thousand drachmas," my father explained, after a few moments of calculation. "If you add the sixty thousand you told me you already have, it will be exactly the sum needed to purchase the olive field at Cambos. That's prime land, with a yield of twenty barrels of olive oil per annum. I guarantee it. The parties involved are my friends. It's an honest-to-goodness deal. All you have to do is come to town tomorrow and sign."

"But what am going I do with an extra field? My good sons are gone to America, and the one left me is useless. Who will take care of the hiring, harvesting, and all the chores? Better hold on to the money."

"That money is not so safe," my father insisted. "You have to deposit it to the bank and change it into Greek drachmas. If the Italians occupy us, it'll become worthless. A field can always be resold later."

Grandfather leaned over the fire, wiping his watery eyes with his handkerchief, weighing the matter. "All right," he said finally. "We'll go to town tomorrow." The decision cheered him up. He stepped out of the kitchen and down to his cellar, coming back a few minutes later, carrying a bottle of his good wine. He opened it by pulling a string he had tied around the cork, which popped out easily.

This was his method of corking his wine bottles. Each New Year's Day, he went down to his cellar and tied a knot on every string. Then he could count the knots when he wanted to know how old one of his wines was. He had wine bottles—and some bottles of rose vinegar—that were as much as twenty-five years old. I had seen his rows of bottles behind his big wine barrels, which he asked me to help him clean once a year when I happened to be at the village at harvest time.

Meanwhile, Grandmother was busy preparing a pot of macaroni, which she seasoned with garlic sauce. She bustled around, getting everybody a plate, toasting slices of bread over the coals, and watching the pot cook.

Vasilis had been invited to stay and was soon enjoying a hearty dinner. Tomorrow, he would have to come back and place more bags with dirt over the planks, he was told. My father explained that the shelter wouldn't be completely finished even then, but in an emergency, it could be used.

"That's why it's sensible to get into that shelter when the raids start," he said to Grandfather.

Just then, Uncle George came in. His face brightened when he saw the food, and Grandmother rushed to serve him a plate.

"Where were you all day?" Grandfather grumbled, seeing him sit down across the table and start eating. "There was work to be done here."

"Didn't you yourself send me to Kosmas's to help get the olives pressed?" Uncle George blurted out, keeping busy with his food. "It was your idea, not mine. Don't have to stay home either."

"I sent for you! Some folks don't ever get things done."

"Leave the boy alone," Grandmother snapped. "Who can jump at one's beck and call all the time? Young people have their rights too. Let him be."

Grandfather shrank back in his seat and chewed his food in mute discontent. Six of us were eating, but there was still plenty of food. Grandmother added salted sardines to the meal, and the bread browned over the coals was tasty too. I was allowed to drink half a glass of watered wine from the bottle Grandfather had opened. He slowly came into a lighter mood as he poured himself glass after glass. His cheeks flamed, and then I discovered that, though he was balding now, he must have been a handsome man in his youth.

"God bless!" he repeated with every sip he took. "Let us win this war. It'll be a shame if the Italians beat us. We're fighting for our lives, aren't we?"

"That's a good thing you did too," my father added, changing the subject. "Makes sense to get that field."

"He's born to purchase things," Grandmother said. "But he couldn't have done it without our sons in America."

"And my son-in-law here to talk sense into me. Money alone can't buy things. You have to have the right stuff up here too." He pointed at his head, casting a sidelong glance at Uncle George, who hadn't said another word since he had come in, not even seeming curious about the purchase of field. "Long live Metaxas!" The old man raised his glass, toasting the dictator prime minister. "He'll lick those bastards. You'll see."

"All right, Christo," Grandmother said to him, touching his elbow. "It's your bedtime."

"One more, one more!" Grandfather insisted. "Let's drink this to Metaxas!"

Tears had come into the old man's eyes, and his emotion made him shake like a leaf.

Grandmother gently pulled him away. “Let’s go, Christo,” she cajoled him. “You shouldn’t have drunk that much wine. Shame on you!”

As she led him to his room, the rest of us sat silent, warming ourselves by the blazing fire, digesting the rich food and drink. I felt so contented, so free from worry. I didn’t mind the odd company or having seen my grandfather drunk.

CHAPTER 3

The Mountain

Next morning, Grandfather sat in his kitchen in front of the fireplace, bleary-eyed and sunken in apathy. He snorted and occasionally spat into the fire; his euphoric mood of last night was totally gone. My father slurped his coffee and explained to Uncle George why he needed to come to town too.

"You have to cosign the papers. After all, that field will belong to you and to your brothers one day."

"I'm not sure about that field. It's too far away, and I'd have to walk ten kilometers to get there. And I don't care what happens one day. My brothers are in America, and I got to do all the chores. All I want is to get married—*now*." He was engaged to a much younger woman from a nearby village, but the war had prevented her folks from going along with the wedding plans.

"No weddings," the old man said, snapping out of his lethargy. "When the war is over, God willing, we'll think about it."

The sound of a horn put an end to the argument.

It was Constantine, the truck owner, who had stopped to pick them up. He was a red-faced man of middle years, known for his terrible swearing habits. This morning, he was blaring insults against the government, irked that he had to go to town to register his truck. All vehicle owners, a news broadcast had said earlier, must report them to the authorities.

"Come on, Constantine," my father said, trying to reassure him half-jokingly. "Your truck is just a collection of loose boards. What's the government going to do with a wreck like that?"

But that dubious comment failed to soothe Constantine's nerves. He cursed one of the saints loudly enough that my grandmother in her kitchen heard him.

She stepped out onto the balcony and shook her finger at him. "Atheist," she scolded him. "Aren't you ashamed to talk like that in front of children?" And she pointed at me.

Constantine gave her a mean look but held his tongue, probably out of deference to his elderly uncle. Grandfather, meanwhile, was being hustled into the front seat of the truck and made to sit uncomfortably between the driver and my father. Uncle George, looking glum, climbed into the open back, where he would have to stand, holding on to one of the rails.

The truck rumbled down the cobblestones and disappeared in the morning fog.

I went back to the kitchen and sat before a dying fire, holding a book. Without Grandfather, the house looked bleak. Grandmother had gone to the basement to do her laundry, too busy to pay much attention to me. From the window, I could see Vasilis, who had come to work; he was carrying bags of dirt on his wheelbarrow to place over the planks in the shelter. I decided that watching such a lonely activity wouldn't keep me entertained. I plunged into a chapter of *Cesar Cascabel*, the Jules Verne novel I had borrowed from my friend Panos. This was the story of a rag-tag group of acrobats who were stranded in Canada after having been robbed of their money. They decided to return to Europe via Alaska and Siberia, crossing the Bering Straits on ice. Their trip was interrupted when they were captured and enslaved by Eskimos. Cascabel, a ventriloquist, was attempting to con the Eskimos into believing that one of their gods had spoken and had given them instructions to let the captive group go.

The suspense rose to a pitch, but I felt restless.

I put the book aside and walked downstairs into the yard. The almond trees in Grandfather's terraced orchard looked bare in late November, their yellow leaves forming a carpet on the dried grass. I saw Grandmother's goat tied to a pole, bleating, lonesome.

Just then I caught sight of my cousin Eleni trotting down the lane, just underneath Grandfather's fence, driving her two goats to pasture. As I watched her, hiding behind the bushes, I had an idea. What if I took Grandmother's goat to pasture myself? I had done that before and knew where to go—just across the valley to a rocky hill used as pasture grounds. I could spend my morning there, killing time, and perhaps have a chance to catch a glimpse of my pretty cousin.

Grandmother gave her consent, provided I held on to the goat's rope safely. "Don't let it wander into the neighbors' vineyards," she cautioned me.

I promised I wouldn't do that, and she sent me off after providing me with a paper bag full of rolls and almonds in case I got hungry out there. She didn't specify a time for my return, but I was probably expected to be back by early afternoon.

I thought I would follow Eleni uphill, but by the time I was ready to get going, she was out of sight. I decided to climb up the hill anyway to see whether I could locate her. I had no idea what I would to do if I came face-to-face with her; I'd probably pretend I hadn't seen her.

The goat pulled ahead, picking ilex leaves from the bushes in the bluffs, not minding the spikes and looking hungrier all the time. This beast could feed an entire day until its belly got bloated on both sides, and then it looked as if it had swallowed balloons. I fully intended to get rid of this pesky animal when I reached Grandfather's field. I'd tie it to a branch and let it graze on the nearby bushes.

I found the entrance and went into Grandfather's vineyard, a half-abandoned piece of property that stretched over an entire slope.

The soil was thin and reddish, mixed with granite splinters that looked like fragments from an underground explosion. The field was sparsely planted with rows of knotty vines that had aged, like Grandfather. This had been a good vineyard in its prime and still gave Grandfather some of his finest wine. The bottle he had opened last night was from that field and that partly explained his jovial mood.

I tied the goat's rope to a branch, giving the animal room enough to graze. I sat on a stone under a leafless carob tree to relish my grandmother's spicy rolls. An hour or so passed, but I had lost the sense of time in the village. Grandfather had only one clock, which sat on top of a chest of drawers in his living room and showed from half an hour to an hour late, so nobody trusted it. Grandfather could tell the time by his roosters crowing in the middle of the night and got up abysmally early to sit before his fire and think his endless, silent thoughts. I still figured I did not know this man. He seemed powerful and weak at the same time, surly, uncompanionable, and cranky with his wife and son, but he could also slide into good moods and palaver for hours, especially when my father was present. Those two had found chemistry between them for reasons that weren't altogether clear to me.

My father was a difficult man too. Though responsible and good-natured, he could hurl a brick at you if you irritated him. He was especially hard on his hired help, from whom he expected perfection; he always complained that his assistants at the sawmill, some of whom were his cousins, fell short of his standards. In any case, he and Grandfather fit like hand in glove. He and the old man could have been father and son, for my father was unhappy with his father (for reasons I cannot state here), and my grandfather was unhappy with his sons. He had several others who had immigrated to America, but besides receiving their checks, he didn't think much of them. In truth, my father and grandfather were both alienated men who found, in each other's company, a small island of mutual appreciation and comradeship.

My thoughts were interrupted by the grating sound of planes. I looked up and saw a squadron of Italian bombers flying over the Bay of Preveza, heading south. I left the goat tied to a tree and started running, intending to gain a small peak ahead of me and see where the bombs dropped. Things were getting noisy too. I heard the explosions and saw dozens of white cotton puffs—anti-aircraft shells bursting between plane formations.

In the next moment, one of the planes was hit by a shell and was nearly cut in half. I saw it all clearly, though it happened miles away. The plane spun in the air, nose-dived, and swooped downward. Cries of joy from workers in the surrounding hills reached my ears.

I thought this was a miracle happening before my eyes, and I ran faster toward the top of the hill to see where the plane had fallen. Soon, I reached the Chapel of Prophet Elias, with its white-washed stone walls and steeple, at the edge of a steep cliff. The Bay of Preveza, the canal, and our town all came into view at once. I stood on the wall, but I could see nothing at all. The plane must have fallen into the sea, too far away. The bombers were gone, and the anti-aircraft guns had ceased firing.

I turned to go back to the goat and found myself face-to-face with Eleni. She stood just a few feet from me on the gravelly surface of the churchyard. Her black eyes shone like coals, and she looked as if she had seen a ghost. She and I stood there for a few seconds, not saying anything.

"Did you see that plane get hit?" I asked.

"What are you doing up here?" she shot back, not answering my question. We were both the same age (about thirteen and a half), but she had almost grown to the size of a woman; she was a good student too. I was short and had let my grades slide lately.

"I brought up my grandfather's goat to graze," I said, my courage abandoning me.

"And where is that goat now?"

"I left it tied to a tree. I ran up here to see where that plane fell."

She seemed unimpressed by my reasons. "You'd better get back there, or there won't be a goat left to find."

I skipped by her hastily and ran in the direction of the vineyard. I covered the short distance through the vineyards in a few minutes, and my cousin's warning proved right, to be sure. There was no sign of the goat. It had jerked the rope loose and was gone—but where? I climbed on a big rock and looked, but the goat hadn't wandered into the heights. Suddenly, I saw it trotting downhill on the path we had come from, bleating loudly, the rope swinging wildly behind it.

I gave chase, but after a minute or two, I realized I wasn't going to catch up with it. The winding track went in opposite directions every hundred yards or so, and it occurred to me that I could overtake the goat if I cut through the terraces and shortened my path. I started scrambling through the vineyards, my legs getting scratched by the bare branches of the vines and my shoes sinking in the soft soil. I had to jump from one terrace to another, and as I attempted to do so from an unusually high one, the whole stone wall, loosened up by the rains, gave way under my weight. I tumbled headlong, with a heap of stones and soil falling on top of me.

When I tried to get up, a sharp pain pierced my left shoulder. I was almost unable to move my left arm, but I managed to stand. The next thing I thought of was the goat. I had to catch it at any cost; otherwise, how could I face my grandmother? She had trusted me with the one animal that provided them with their daily milk. Grandfather liked a little white cheese with his meals. This was the animal that gave it.

I continued to stumble down walls, falling two or three more times, but I finally got ahead of the goat and faced it as it was coming down, bleating wildly. I blocked its passage and grabbed the rope. There was no question of taking it back to pasture. The pain stabbed my left shoulder, and I had to get back home.

I saw Constantine's truck, huffing uphill and making a right turn toward the village. It had only two passengers—Grandfather and Uncle George, who leaned out of the window when he saw me.

"Your father sends word that you go back to town tomorrow," he said. "Your school has started."

CHAPTER 4

The Healer

I developed a high fever during the night, and in the morning, my grandmother decided it was impossible for me to make the trip to town. My left shoulder was swollen and intensely painful. She put hot compresses on it and a plaster of boiled herbs, and those eased the pain, but I wasn't feeling much better. By midmorning, Grandmother had sent word to my father that I was ill and couldn't be moved. My father arrived early in the afternoon, having waited to take one of the two buses that still operated in wartime. His face was haggard. I knew this look very well; he'd wear it every time something went wrong, especially something concerning his son, whose welfare mattered to him more than anything else in the world.

"How is he?" he asked my grandmother.

"Just a little better," she said falsely, just to reassure him. Since morning, I had actually felt worse.

"What is it?"

"His left shoulder bothers him. He says he fell from a terrace while chasing the goat he took to the mountain yesterday. He asked me permission to do that, and I gave it, thinking it was a nice way for him to spend the day."

I detected a little guilt in her voice, but Father seemed not to be paying much attention to her. As usual, his energetic mind was already looking for a way to get me to a doctor or to find a doctor who would come here. In wartime, this wasn't so easy. In the whole northern part of the island, there was only one doctor, who had to be transported to the various villages constantly, on mule or horse, to see patients. It was doubtful that Father could find him, but he, of course, had no alternative but to send for him. Vasilis, always willing to do errands (for a payment, of course), was dispatched to bring the doctor, but he came back forty-five minutes later to announce that Dr. Katsenos had gone to a distant village and wouldn't be back until tomorrow.

"What are we to do?" Grandmother said, wringing her hands. "The boy is suffering. His temperature is rising. He'll die without help."

All this was said in my presence, with no regard for my feelings. But I was in agony and feverish, and whatever passed in those moments only partly registered. I was the one who was dying, so what was the point of not telling me?

"Take him to Yannakos," Vasilis's wife said. She had come in the meantime, along with a few other women of the neighborhood.

"He is a quack," my father said. He had a poor opinion of country medicine men who practiced all sorts of cures. But this time, he had no alternative. A practical doctor was better than leaving me there without any help.

Vasilis brought his donkey again, and they helped me on it, making me ride side-saddle for greater comfort. As the afternoon had turned drizzly, they placed an overcoat over my head. It was a ride of about three kilometers, and it was all sheer misery. My shoulder was inflamed, I had hot flashes, and the pain was so sharp that I thought my shoulder was being wrenched off. The only thing that kept me brave was the miserable sight of my father, who walked alongside the donkey, his hand on my back to support me. This iron man, who was rarely defeated by anything, now looked crushed. The anxiety printed on his face was so deep it almost made me forget my own misery.

We arrived at Yannakos's house in about half an hour. He was a man in his late sixties, with white hair, a bulbous nose, and kindly eyes. He sat on a wheelchair with wooden wheels, his legs covered by a blanket. It didn't take me long to realize he was paralyzed from the waist down. But that did not impede the movement of his supple hands. As soon as he touched my shoulder and softly massaged the swollen area, I knew that he was a healer.

His examination lasted about five minutes, and then he said, "The shoulder is dislocated. I'll have to set it." He rubbed the affected area with warm olive oil, which his wife, a woman of sixty-five or so, brought him in a saucer. Then, softening his voice to give me courage, he said, "This is going to be a bit stinging, my boy, and you'll have to brace yourself. But don't worry, the pain will be gone immediately afterward."

I clenched my teeth and prepared for the shock. He took my left arm by the biceps, held the upper part of my shoulder blade with the other, and jerked the arm forcefully in his direction—or at least, that's what I thought happened because the pain was so sharp that I fainted.

When I came to, lying on Aunt Angelika's bed (I forgot to tell you that she was one of my father's aunts), the sharp pain in my shoulder was almost gone. Yannakos had put a plaster like a giant Band-Aid on my shoulder, and soon, I felt comfortable enough to move. Then they helped me put my shirt back on, and he put my arm in a sling. I didn't have to go back to see him, he said. I'd feel much better soon.

My father handed Yannakos five ten-drachma coins—at that time, a good payment—and then added an extra one for good measure. He felt sorry for old folks in the villages, who, with the young people gone to the front, had no means of support and who probably would end up dying of starvation. Cruel days lay ahead, he said.

Yannakos placed the money inside a handkerchief, tying it in a knot. He probably would keep this large sum for an emergency. I had seen peasants do that all the time. Real money rarely came their way; they mostly subsisted on vegetables from their backyard plots.

The ride back was quiet. Though I was still uncomfortable, the pain had lessened considerably. When we got back to Grandfather's,

Grandmother had prepared bean soup, which was a godsend for my empty stomach—as soon as my pain had eased, my appetite had returned. My father ate too, happy to see me feeling better. He stayed there overnight, and in the morning, he took me with him on Constantine's truck. My hand still was in the sling. It would have to stay like that for a few days, I was told. But my dreaded return to school had already obliterated yesterday's anxieties.

CHAPTER 5

Back to School

I stayed home in bed for a couple of days. My mother gave me nutritious food, so with less pain and a healthy diet, I felt comfortable and warm and had a chance to read a couple more chapters of the Verne book. Soon, I learned that Katia had left for Gytheion, and Stathis himself had applied for a transfer to Athens, where he would seek to get some politician to have his fiancée join him there. I heard him ask my father if he could get him a gallon bottle of olive oil, which my father had stored in a back room along with other agricultural products for the duration of the war.

"I'll pay you in cash," Stathis said.

"Forget about that," my father responded. "I know that man. I bribed him myself to get you your job here. He is slippery. He takes the bribes and then forgets to do what he promised. Better get half a dozen British gold coins; they sell them in the black market."

Stathis mumbled that his teacher's salary wouldn't allow him to do that, and my father told him to sell some of his expensive suits to get the money, knowing his brother's extravagant habits, which he often criticized.

I liked Stathis, who had been helping me with my algebra exercises and my Latin or other subjects. When he heard that I was ill, he went out hunting, and when he came in early in the afternoon, still in his hunter's outfit, he showed me two dead thrushes that he had brought back from his hunting trip. He let me touch the birds, big and fat and still warm in my hands. Later, my mother roasted them on the spit, and I had a good slice of one of them, a delicious dinner that put me in a still-better mood that evening. *Why can't I stay a few more days like this?* I thought as I turned on my good shoulder and went to sleep.

In the morning, I went back to school. My mother wanted me to stay in bed another day, but Stathis opined that my cheeks looked rosy enough (probably that came after I had eaten some leftovers from his thrushes for breakfast), and my father agreed with him. For once, I saw him looking less depressed about my illness. "It wasn't my feet that ached," he murmured to himself, "just my arm." I could keep that in the sling. Meanwhile, I might attend classes.

I walked to school, not too happy. My first two classes were the apex of tedium: Professor Sordatos, an older professor (Perdakaris had been drafted), explained a passage from the *Apology* of Socrates, but what he said was translated words and syntax and had little to do with the meaning. I saw others yawning. I was still groggy from two easy days in bed, so I yawned too. My shoulder still bothered me a bit.

During the second hour, I was taught algebra—equations of the second degree—by a replacement of Chufas's, who had been called up and joined the fighting forces in Albania. This teacher was a bent old fellow who had been mobilized to teach, although he'd been retired for ten years. After seeing my grandfather, a real personality who had his moments of vigor, this fellow looked like an emptied bedbug, muttering and cackling, though his eyes were kind, and later I heard he had been a good teacher in his prime. But my brain, due to long abstinence from use, had grown too sluggish to grasp the elaborate symbols he laid out on the blackboard. Later, I decided that I had been hasty in my judgment of him, a man who, after all, had tried, in his old age, to do his patriotic duty and educate his country's youth.

I noticed Eleni was back, and during the break, I saw her with Panos in a tête-à-tête in the corner of the yard. He gave me a meaningful stare in which I detected his irritation at my growing curiosity. I thought about the bargain we had struck and whether he would let me keep the Verne book. He always wrangled with me; I could keep the book provided I took a message to my cousin. Feeling rejected and inferior, I didn't behave politely.

Back in the classroom, I felt uncomfortable with sitting stiffly for hours on the wooden bench, and my shoulder pierced me several times, especially after Chalimourdas, a tall, rustic-looking fellow sitting next to me, gave me a shove.

I was restless and tired all morning, and when I returned home for lunch, I told my mother I was too ill to go back for my afternoon classes. Without argument, my mother served me lunch and then took me upstairs to bed and told me to stay there. Tasoula, a neighborhood medicine woman, came with a balm consisting of boiled walnut leaves. The leaves were still steaming when she placed them under my arm. Then she said a prayer, took her coffee in the hall (there were no visiting women today), and left. She often read coffee cups to worried mothers whose sons served in the war and collected good coin for her services.

I couldn't read the Verne book, as much as I wanted to, because I was in pain. The compress had done no good, and neither had Tasoula's home remedy. When Stathis came in, he recommended that my father send for Grigoris, the famous town doctor, saying that he and the doctor were pals. My father asked him to fetch the doctor himself. Half an hour later, Stathis came back with Dr. Grigoris, a tall, imposing man with fair skin, wavy dark-blond hair, and a tone of authority in his voice.

Dr. Grigoris said little, but his words carried weight. He examined my shoulder carefully for five minutes or so, took my pulse and temperature, used his stethoscope to listen to my chest and back, and then said, "The shoulder's dislocated and badly set."

"What can we do?" my father asked.

"For the moment, not much. I'll give him a shot to kill the pain, and then you give him an aspirin every four hours. There's no way that we can reset the bone into its socket. It will make everything worse. He could have an operation, but that will require a trip to Patras and much expense."

"Is he going to be all right?"

"The shoulder will heal, but it will take some time."

"How long?"

"May be a year … or two."

"Am I going to be in pain, Doctor?" I asked.

Grigoris looked at me. He had kind eyes—eyes that inspired confidence in a patient. "Not for long. But you must avoid moving the arm up and down. Keep it in the sling, and do as little as you can with it."

My mother had come in and was listening to the doctor's words carefully. I thought I could see a faint blush in her cheeks.

Grigoris prepared his syringe and got ready to give me the injection. I felt a shiver inside me and a momentary faintness. The sting was sharp, but not as horrible as I thought it would be.

"And keep those phony women away from him," I heard the doctor say to my uncle as soon as they were out the door. "He doesn't need more plasters or steam baths. The bone is all right; it will set by itself."

When the two men came back into the room, I saw that my father had been reassured by the doctor's words. I was out of any immediate danger, and that was the most important thing, he said to my uncle. In that sense, both brothers were similar: neither of them could stand uncertainty and went to pieces every time something went wrong.

As soon as they were out of the room, I fell into a deep coma-like sleep, and when I awoke, the pain had numbed. It was near evening, and my mother brought me supper—a slice of liver that she had roasted over the coals, a tasty and nutritious meal. Father and Stathis came in, but my eyes remained unfocused as I gazed at them briefly before lapsing back into sleep.

In the morning I felt much better than the day before, so I asked my mother to let me go to school. I hated staying in that bed and having to hear the constant buzz of visitors who poured in. Aunt Agatha, my grandmother's sister, had arrived with her youngest son, a boy of twelve, who, she said, had developed a swollen foot after having stepped on a rusted nail and needed medical attention.

"But we already have a sick one in the house," my mother protested—she had always thought Aunt Agatha was a pest.

"We only need to stay a day or two," Agatha pleaded. "We don't have anywhere else to go."

"Can't Andrew put you up?" That was her oldest son, a baker, who had a job in town and who, at one time, used to live with us. I had taken over the room he had rented; I slept and did all my schoolwork there.

"He's only renting a small place, and he doesn't have an extra bed. Can't we have his room?"

"No!" my mother cried. Her face had turned purple, and it seemed to me she gasped for breath. "That's my son's room."

I left them arguing as I stepped into the yard, where Agatha's son, Zois, waited, still sitting on their donkey. I said hello to Zois, a wild-looking boy with small eyes and long, uncombed hair that reminded me of a porcupine I had once seen near a bush in the village.

Today, I didn't find the lessons hard or tedious. For one thing, the first class was geography, and my constant reading of Verne stories had given me a head start on that subject. Stathis had a good library, and sometimes I sneaked into his room while he was away, picked a book from his bookcase, read parts of it, and placed it back after bending the page to mark my progress.

Eleni was sitting last in the third row of girls to my right. I turned my eyes to her several times, but she persistently avoided meeting my glance. I found her maddeningly unfriendly, even aloof.

The next class was ancient history, the Battle of Marathon, where outnumbered Athenians had defeated a much-larger invading Persian force. It was taught by Professor Giannoulis, a short, fat fellow who was nicknamed "the Penguin" (I heard this from Stathis during dinnertime). The professor used a lot of pompous words, like *stupendous* and *incredible*, trying to impress his class. He was a good teacher, though, and despite his mannerisms, I learned from him.

During lunch break, I headed home, as usual. Panos did the same thing, and he soon joined me.

"I see you're feeling better," he said, speaking to me for the first time since I returned to school.

"I'm fine," I said rather coldly. Since he had bargained with me the other day about the Verne book, I didn't like him as much anymore.

"Listen," he said, sounding contrite. "I hope you forget what I said the other day."

"Forget what, exactly?" Of course, I knew what he meant, but I pretended indifference, just to spite him.

"About carrying a note to your cousin. She's a girl I truly respect. I don't want her good name smeared."

"I don't care about her good name. She's nothing to me."

"I thought you did care."

"Well, I don't."

He said nothing else for a minute or two—we walked silently side by side—and then he said, "I'm afraid you have to return that book tonight."

"You said I could keep it until the end of the week."

"I know, but my father says the book must be given back. He complains that I've let too many of my friends borrow his books, and his library's dwindling. He's lost several good books already."

His father was a leather merchant, quite well-to-do, and to display his wealth, he had purchased a gramophone, a rare thing in town those days. He invited us boys to his house and taught us how to dance the tango. He did a good job with us youngsters, although he was almost completely deaf.

"But you aren't going to lose it. We are next door neighbors. I'll give it to you in three days."

"I'm afraid you have to return it tonight."

"The hell with you!" I said furiously. "And here's your book." I opened my school bag, which I carried on my healthy shoulder, and gave him the Jules Verne book. I had taken it along with my school books, hoping to read a page or two during recess or even during class, so I could return it as soon as possible.

"You can keep it until tonight."

"No, take it." I handed it to him and ran away from him.

"I hope we can stay friends," Panos called after me.

"Not you and me."

When I got home, I found out that Agatha had settled in, having been given the room upstairs that I used as a bedroom and study. Now, I would return to my parents' bedroom, where there was an extra bed and where I had slept during my illness. I personally didn't mind that accommodation, but I saw that my mother was sore. She had resisted Agatha's staying with us until my father, who had come home for his midmorning cup of coffee, heard Agatha's groans and saw the boy's condition. He said they could stay for a few days.

My mother, usually kind-faced, looked out of sorts as she served me a plain meal—lentil soup with brown bread and a piece of white cheese. Zois was upstairs, sleeping in my room, and Agatha had gone out to the bakery to find her son Andrew to ask him for money.

I finished my meal and started back for school, but as I stepped out of the house, sounds of church bells chiming in a chorus came to my ears. I started running, and when I reached the school, I saw Stephan, one of my classmates, standing outside the gate, waving his hands in the air.

"Tepeleni was taken!" he shouted. "Long live Greece!"

It was another victory in Albania.

CHAPTER 6

The Sick Boy

Tepeleni was the third Albanian town that the Greek army had taken from the Italians in a month! The bells chimed all afternoon, and crowds gathered outside cafés to hear the radio broadcasts. People laughed, joked, and clapped hands every time a news bulletin came on.

After school, I roamed into the main street as far as the local barbershop, where a man outside distributed candy—a paste made of sugar, almonds, and egg whites. It was wrapped in cellophane, and it stuck to my fingers and later to my teeth. But it was so delicious, I didn't mind chewing it! All afternoon, the bells continued to chime, although a couple of times the sirens blared, and planes passed overhead. But by now, people were used to these warnings and ignored them, knowing the bombs fell on the Bay of Preveza.

War or no war, winning had emboldened people with the belief of invincibility. My father said this was foolish, and he kept digging holes inside the walls that could be used as shelters in an emergency. Once or twice, he fit me into one, saying I should stay there until the sirens stopped. It was dark, as the room was filled with lumber, and soon I had palpitations, couldn't breathe, and started screaming. My father pulled me out, and my mother helped me lie on a sofa and put a compress soaked in cold aromatic vinegar on my head. They put me in bed for a while and gave me a pill to calm me down, but it was hours before I could get up.

That evening, we had several guests for dinner. In addition to Agatha and her sick son (his mother took a plate to him upstairs), in came Stathis with his buddy Andrew, who wanted to inquire after his sick brother and stayed for dinner. Andrew and Stathis had turned out to be goods pals, though their social standings were incompatible: Stathis, a high school teacher and a civil servant, went with the elite crowd—architects, lawyers, teachers, and Grigoris, the doctor. Andrew was practically uneducated and worked as a hired hand in a local bakery. It was a hard life for him, for he had to get up at three in the morning to knead bread and shovel hundreds of loaves in and out of the hot oven. But his mother said she was grateful he had a job in town and escaped being a peasant.

My mother had prepared beef stew with onions. She sliced the meat into tiny bits and poured sauce over a large platter of spaghetti so that there would be enough food for everybody. Luckily, Andrew had brought a couple of loaves from the bakery, so at least bread was plentiful.

Stathis had a cold and sneezed constantly, but that didn't stop him from talking excitedly about the fall of Tepeleni. He had brought along with him an extra edition of the daily paper, which had just arrived from Athens, announcing the event in large print. A cartoon on the front page showed Mussolini running away from a kilted Greek footman, who had stuck his bayonet in the dictator's rear. I asked Stathis if he'd let me clip out that cartoon, and he promised me I could have it later.

The mailman arrived, holding two letters, both for Stathis. One was from Katia, announcing that her application to be transferred to Athens had been approved and that she was moving there in a couple of weeks. That made Stathis jump for joy—but his second letter said that his own application for Athens had been turned down. His services in the civil defense, it said, were indispensable to our town.

"That seems reasonable to me," said my father. "After the war, you can go there. I have that politician in my pocket."

But that did not soothe Stathis's mood; he sat down in a sneezing fit and then left the room abruptly.

The meal ground to a stop, except for Agatha, whose appetite grew with every bite. She soon emptied a second plate of spaghetti and wiped her dish clean with a chunk of bread. My mother took the platter to refill it in the kitchen but left it there.

My father thought it might be a good idea to send for Grigoris, who was still in town, when Stathis came back down. He sat at the table, and my mother brought him a plate with some chunks of meat that had survived Agatha's voracity. Stathis finished his meal and then said goodnight and withdrew. Andrew left too, and Agatha stayed downstairs to help my mother with the dishes.

I turned to some of my algebra exercises, something I hadn't done in a long time, but nothing stuck in my memory. The terrifying moments at the shelter had ruined my evening. I asked my mother for another pill, and she gave me one, and I swallowed it. Bitter or not, it must have helped me to sleep.

Next day, Stathis did not go to school but stayed in bed to nurse his cold. I went, but I was in a bad mood because the first class was algebra, and I hadn't prepared last night—and besides, I didn't have the Verne book on my knees to read surreptitiously, as I did when the topic was boring. I returned home midafternoon and found my mother and Agatha sitting together upstairs, in the corridor near the balcony. Tasoula sat next to them on a stool, reading the dregs in a coffee cup. That absorbed my mother's attention too, and for a moment, she seemed to have forgotten her worries.

I knocked on Stathis's door to check if he had clipped out the cartoon of Mussolini that he had promised me. He was in bed, looking sick, but when he saw me at the door, he asked me to come in.

"Listen," he said in a lowered voice. (I couldn't understand why he didn't want to be heard.) "I'm going to ask you to do me a little favor."

"Of course," I said. I was ready to oblige him.

"I want you to go out and mail this letter for me. I can't go anywhere tonight. I have a fever."

He looked in bad shape, so I said I would.

"I have your Mussolini," he added, handing me the clipped cartoon—so he hadn't forgotten his promise. He gave me the letter and a two-drachma coin.

"Thanks," I murmured as I took it.

It was good to have some change in my pocket. I told my mother where I was going and went outside, intending to make as large a round through town as I could to kill time. I didn't want to study, and the house with Zois and Agatha in it—plus my sick uncle--was more like a hospital than a home. The siren howled a couple of times, giving me palpitations, but I tried to steady myself and finish my errand.

I looked at the letter and saw it was addressed to Katia in Athens. I wondered what that meant, but after I mailed it, my thoughts turned to the two-drachma coin in my pocket. I didn't want to spend it on candy. Perhaps I could see if I could buy the Verne book for myself, rather than be obligated to that spoiled Panos, whose father had money. I'd gotten tired of begging him. But for the moment, I just saved the money and hoped for more tips from Stathis to add to my little nest egg.

When I returned home, the doctor had arrived to examine Zois's hurting foot. It was badly bandaged with rags, and as he took these off, I could see fluid ooze out of his heel, and his foot was swollen to the size of a gourd. It was turning brownish—a horrible hue—and smelled like rotten meat.

"Hmm ... very bad," Grigoris said, almost immediately. Then he took my father aside and said in a low tone (though I was close enough to hear him), "Gangrene has set in. You must take the boy right away to a hospital in Patras. The foot has to be amputated. If this is not done now, the entire leg will rot, and then there could be no chance of saving him. Even now, it might be too late."

My father communicated the news to Agatha, who started moaning and cursing her luck in a loud voice. "How can I do that? I have no money in the world, and my son won't give me a penny, the scrooge!"

I could tell my father was thinking, and I knew he had already made up his mind to do something for the destitute widow and her boy. His eyebrows were twitching, and his hand was rubbing against his stubble—he shaved at the local barber's only twice a week—a sign that he was about to take matters into his own hands.

"We'll take the boy to Patras tonight," he said, without much hesitation

I saw my mother's thunderstruck look.

My father lost no time and went to find Andrew, who worked at a nearby bakery. When Andrew heard the news about what Dr. Grigoris had said, he took off his baker's apron and tossed it on a bench. He told his boss he had an emergency at home and then followed my father to the harbor to inquire about the Corfu–Patras line. They were told that *Pylaros*, a prewar liner still making that route, was due in Patras in a couple of hours. Andrew bought two tickets—one for himself and one for his sick brother. My father bought a ticket for himself, having decided to go along to help them.

He and my mother had an argument. She said that during a war, a trip by boat—the only way to get there—was a death trap, with all the mines floating in the sea, set up by the Germans and Italians to sink English warships. Steam liners and fishing boats obtained permission to navigate through passing lanes, but one never knew when a stray mine would hit and blow up a civilian ship—and it had happened.

But my father was adamant. "This is an emergency," he said. "A boy's life is at stake. What if your son [me] was in the same situation?"

She gave in but not without a deep sigh.

They left early that afternoon, carrying the boy on a stretcher. Zois was in good spirits, seemingly not in too much in pain and not very alarmed that he had to travel. When Agatha saw her son being carried away, she wept and tore at her cheeks as if she were at his funeral. She thought she would never see her boy alive again. She insisted on going with the men, but Andrew convinced her she must stay behind.

"A wailing woman will be of no use on dangerous trip," Andrew told my father.

Both men assured Agatha that Zois's illness was not serious and that they would all be back home soon. The three went on board the *Pylaros*, and I saw my father on the deck, waving his straw hat to my mother, who stood on the wharf with Agatha and me. My mother blew her nose into her handkerchief and turned her face away from me. I felt sorry for her and took her hand as we started back home.

It was a dreary, cloudy midafternoon, and when we arrived back home, she got busy preparing a snack to steady our spirits. She soaked bread in water; sprinkled it with oregano, drops of olive oil, and vinegar; and added feta cheese, fresh tomatoes, salted sardines, and boiled eggs. We all ate in silence. Agatha, usually loquacious, kept her thoughts to herself. The rest of the day passed in dull silence.

CHAPTER 7

The Fortune Teller

While my father, Andrew, and the sick boy were away, a routine was established for the rest of us. I found life duller than usual. Stathis was sneezing and grumpy, but he went back to his duties at school. A couple of days later, he gave me another two-drachma coin to take a second letter to Katia. I didn't know why, but he looked gloomy, almost desperate. He also had a letter from Chufas, who said he had frostbite and had been transferred to Athens for treatment.

When I was home from school, I sat at my desk and did my homework in silence. Afternoons were quieter than mornings as the daily air raids continued. Always, like clockwork, at eleven in the morning, the sirens sounded as bombs were dropped over Preveza and anti-aircraft shells puffed up in the air.

No bombs were dropped on our town, so people got used to that routine and went out shopping and doing other business. My father always warned us—and me, in particular—to get to the bomb shelters inside the walls, but after what happened to me last time, my mother insisted only that I get under a bed, which I did. When in school, we all went to the basement, quietly and in good order, as Stathis had, by now, trained us to remain disciplined during the air raids.

At home, Mother finished her daily chores by the middle of the afternoon and then sat in the guest room with Agatha for a cup of coffee and a survey of the events of the day.

Agatha sat on a cot that she used as a bed, sofa, and recliner. She talked about her son constantly. Nobody could prevail on her to change the subject. The anxiety about her sick boy fed on her mind during the entire twenty-four hours. She hardly slept and barely touched any food. Her face, deeply lined and distorted with pain, showed her dismal mental state. And she never stopped voicing her fears. The house echoed with her loud talk, and her laments and cries could be heard throughout the neighborhood.

I tried to do my homework when I arrived home from school, but eventually, I was affected and felt deeply sorry for the destitute widow.

To ease her suffering, my mother invited the neighborhood women for a visit and a chat with Agatha during the afternoon hours. The women offered various opinions about Zois's illness, most of which were favorable predictions. Naturally, Tasoula joined these sessions, reading one cup after another and making countless predictions for the mothers who had sons at the front; she almost always offered positive news.

Agatha was aroused by Tasoula's presence and listened to her words with growing interest. It was the best thing to revive her spirits, especially when an entire chorus of women around her gave out exclamations—"Oh! Ah!"—every time Tasoula's enigmatic expressions were heard. Few made sense of them, but it didn't matter, for sometimes it was better to be confused and hopeful than clear-headed and miserable.

Before leaving for Patras, Andrew had left his mother a handful of change so Agatha could afford to pay the fortune teller to read the dregs of her coffee cup, although it was my mother who provided the coffee, cookies, and other treats for these sessions, some of which lasted for hours.

Two days after the men left, a telegram came, saying that the trip went well and that the doctors were examining the boy. Another telegram came a few days later. It urged Agatha to have courage and promised further news soon. A week passed. Then a letter came, indicating that the boy was critically ill. This last piece of news so unnerved Agatha that she had a notion to get on the boat and leave for Patras immediately. She feared her son was near death. My mother was barely able to convince her to stay put and wait for better news.

To help her calm down, she invited Tasoula for a special session that afternoon. I witnessed the whole thing, as it was late in the day, and I had come back from school. I had read the letter from Patras and was fully aware of what was going on.

Tasoula was glowing in her sense of importance as she glided in like an enormous cotton ball. She sat on the cot, which creaked under her weight, took her coffee and sweets, ate, and then placed the cup upside down on a saucer to dry. Agatha sat on my mother's stool, waiting anxiously.

The reading began in about ten minutes—it took that long for the coffee-cup dregs to dry. Then she offered a few conventional wishes, such as continued health for the lady concerned, her family, and all her friends and relatives. This time, Tasoula was unusually ceremonious. She twisted the cup sideways several times, then up and down, making sure the dregs had settled and dried completely. She read prayers from a yellow booklet she carried in her pocket, invoking names of saints: Saint Anargyros, the miracle-doer; Saint Onufrios, the helper of the lame; and others. At the same time, she made the sign of the cross, holding the holy text directly over the cup with her left hand. Then she took the cup and started examining it intently. All the women—most of them had gathered on this occasion—leaned forward.

"I see a shape like a triangle," Tasoula began. "Another shape is here, next to a horizontal line. This is a long line. Then another triangle—a big, big triangle!"

"What does it mean?" Agatha asked breathlessly, hardly comprehending what a triangle was.

"Then another triangle—how sharp!" Tasoula continued exuberantly, without answering. "Holy Ghost! I have never seen such a thing before in my life. Five triangles! And look at this long line going around the rim. This line is never broken by anything. How miraculous! Here! The line reaches the big dot! See?" All eyes followed her finger as it moved around the inside of the cup, stopping before a large, half-dried smudge of dregs.

"What does it mean?" Agatha asked again.

"It means your son is sitting up. He was lying down for a long time—the horizontal line says that. But now he is sitting up. This is a good sign. Your son will be well. This other line"—she pointed to the same line—"shows that he is proceeding to take a long trip—a long, long one; that is, the one coming home. This dot here is you, waiting to receive him." Tasoula ended her prediction with triumph in her voice.

Agatha gave out a loud cry of joy. Her eyes shone, tears ran down her cheeks, and she smiled for the first time in weeks. My mother seemed deeply moved too. Tasoula's words had proven to be a tonic for the women, all of whom seemed in revived spirits and talked about the return of the boy as a sure thing. No coffee-cup reading had ever been so conclusive. It was a God-sent prophecy, with the blessings of the saints. The boy was coming home; they all knew that. Were Tasoula's predictions ever in doubt? The excited women tipped the fortune teller generously, inviting her to come to their homes for readings; they all had their problems, and they all could use some useful advice and a pep talk. They went away, talking to each other and making plans.

Tasoula also received a large fee from my mother and an extra-large one from Agatha, who took her to the door with tears in her eyes. The fortune teller rolled down the stairs and out into the street.

I watched her from the balcony as she stopped to count the coins she had collected. I knew all her predictions were phony, and I recalled Cesar Cascabel trying to con the Eskimos. He, at least, had better motives.

Father arrived later that same afternoon. He came out of the steamboat *Pylaros* and walked all the way home, carrying his suitcase. I saw Mother give a start when she saw him at the doorstep so unexpectedly. His straw hat was tilted slightly backwards over his head, and his eyes were sad and serious. She did not have to ask him for the news from Patras. She knew, just by the look on his face, that the boy had died.

Andrew arrived only moments later and, not saying a word to the rest of us, went straight to his mother. Her lamentations continued all evening and through the night. My mother called Father Spyridon, our local parish priest, and asked him to perform the services for the funeral, which would take place next day. Andrew paid for the expenses, but my father chipped in, buying the casket from a local casket-maker. It had to be small, and for the measurements, they took my height and measured my waist. The funeral itself was to be at the village; Constantine's truck was the mode of transportation. I joined my father and mother in going to the village. Aunt Agatha, wrapped in a black headcover and still wailing loudly, sat in the front with Andrew.

When we reached the village chapel at the top of a hill, I stood around with the others. All present took turns going to the casket and kissing the dead boy's forehead. When my turn came, I noticed that Zois's body, smaller than mine, left empty spaces on the sides of the wooden casket, and black cloth had been stuffed inside to fill the spaces. I crossed myself, leaned forward, and kissed Zois on the forehead. It was cold as ice. That was my first encounter with death.

CHAPTER 8

War Disruptions

It was now mid-December, and we were preparing for the holidays but were in low sprits. The progress at the front had stalled, as after the victory at Tepeleni, the Italians had reinforced their positions and were putting up a staunch resistance. Besides, the winter in the Albanian mountains had been so brutal that victims of frostbite were filling the hospitals in the rear, not to mention the large number of injured. The early spirit of enthusiasm had been dampened, as people began to fear the Germans would soon attack.

Things at home had changed too. My father's parents returned to our town from Ithaca, where my grandfather, the priest, had been officiating for the last decade or so. He suffered from Parkinson's disease, and the shaking of his right hand disqualified him from administering the Holy Communion. When they arrived in early December, new accommodations had to be made after the town had been bombed and lots of private property destroyed, though, luckily, only a few persons were injured or killed. Ironically, one of those killed—torn to pieces by the gasses of the bomb blast—was a woman, a German language instructor to the children of a wealthy merchant near the harbor.

Most of the population moved out of town to the large olive grove west of it and at the edge of the mountain range, where a large cave served as hospital, storage room, and shelter when the sirens sounded. Stathis informed us that was where they had brought the Italian pilot after his plane had been downed earlier. One of his legs was broken, and he had multiple injuries that required medical attention. An angry mob outside the cave hospital shouted and wanted to lynch him, but Stathis stopped the angry crowd, citing the Geneva Convention, which protects prisoners of war. Eventually, the pilot was moved to a hospital in the rear, where he would be treated.

After the bombing, my father moved the lot of us to the village, where my maternal grandfather let us occupy his old house, only a hundred yards or so from his current residence. He still used it to store his big wine barrels in the basement, but the upstairs, with a large sitting room and two bedrooms at the back could accommodate our enlarged family. The floor was full of holes, but my father worked a couple of days to fix them and to replace the broken glass in the windows. The house was still cold at night, and the fire was lit only at an outside stable, where we gathered to cook, eat, and stay warm.

I didn't like my current life one bit. My hands were constantly freezing, my hours were empty, and there were no books (except some of my textbooks) to entertain me. Sheer misery.

But in about a week or so, things changed. My father sent me a message that I was needed in town. Stathis had failed to be transferred and was still there, and Andrew had moved in, bringing several loaves of bread instead of paying rent—our family could use the extra bread, which I had to carry to the village once or twice a week, mostly on foot. I was also useful in other ways. My father brought some fish, cabbage, and potatoes, and he asked me to cook these for our meals—his, mine, and Andrew's. Stathis ate out with his friends, but he occasionally joined us.

Well, I wasn't a cook, nor ever wished to be, but practice makes perfect—well, serviceable, at least. I peeled and sliced the potatoes and fried them in the pan and used other kitchen utensils my mother had left behind. I boiled the vegetables and even cleaned and fried the fish. If nothing else, I had to eat too, and, with a little practice, I became a cook, and three or four males sat down to dinner.

Stathis bought some cheap wine, and that helped lighten the mood of otherwise lonely males. There was a tavern nearby, owned by Milios, a joker and gossip of the neighborhood, who entertained us with his tales. My father told him that his mouth would get him into trouble one day. But Milios couldn't be stopped, and my father decided I shouldn't hear all the details of womanizing males and "loose" women's practices. I was to remain a cook for the duration, he said.

As soon as Panos heard I was back in town, he started shadowing me. Since the bombs fell, Eleni had been in the village, of course, and Panos was overwhelmed with anxiety for her. I told him I had not seen her, except once, when she was driving her goats to pasture.

"Does she wear mittens?" he asked. "Her fingers must be freezing."

"Couldn't see. She was too far off."

"Her father is a criminal. I'm going to write him a letter."

"Listen," I said. "Come to your senses. This is war. Bombs are falling in the city. Do you want her to be here and get killed? When the war is over, she'll be back, like all other students from the villages."

"Will you give her a message from me when you get up there?"

I promised I would—to get rid of him—and he said the Verne book was at my disposal. I accepted his offer. I got the book back, and that brightened my days and the dismal evenings a bit.

Just before Christmas, as my father and I were getting ready to go to the village and rejoin the family for a few days and celebrate there, we had a big surprise. Katia and Achilles Chufas came from Athens to visit Stathis, who was as surprised to see them, as was everyone else.

They went upstairs to the room Stathis occupied and shut themselves in there for many hours. I cooked a meal for them that night, but they all left in a hurry and went to the Averoff Hotel, which had a plush restaurant that still was functioning. After dinner, Stathis came home, but he was uncommunicative, and the next morning, he left in a hurry to rejoin them. It was late afternoon when he came home—he had escorted them to the harbor, where the two boarded *Pylaros* and were gone.

I was puzzled and extremely curious to learn what had happened, but I couldn't get a word from him or from my father. A few days later, Stathis was preparing to leave too, and I saw my father give him a four-gallon can of olive oil and some money from his savings; then he helped Stathis carry his things to the harbor. Before they left the house, Stathis gave me a big hug, with tears in his eyes.

"Goodbye, Uncle," I said, tearful and shocked, realizing that something terrible must be happening to him.

"Goodbye, old buddy," he said. "Carry on with your work and get straight A's next time school opens. And keep a diary. You will never forget these days. See you later."

I never saw him again during the four-year war, and he never wrote to me. I asked my father what had happened, but he wouldn't tell me a word. He said I was too young to hear, but I got some details from Andrew, who liked the meals I cooked for him; he and I were becoming fast friends. He revealed that Katia was leaving Stathis and had returned his engagement ring. She was going to marry Chufas instead. Stathis had left for Athens to get the politician to transfer him there, still hopeful that the fickle Katia would change her mind.

"I hate that stupid mathematician who can't even finish a sentence!" I exploded. I was furious to hear that my beloved uncle, who had encouraged me to become a good student, was hurting.

"Don't say I told you," Andrew said. "They're adults. They'll figure things out."

Christmas up in the mountains was bleak, and so was the New Year. We had good meals, though. My grandfather Christos opened a couple of bottles of his good wine, and we all sat around his big table and ate heartily. There was some cheer there, but the constant drizzle and even snowflakes chilled the momentary good mood that came during those meals.

But the New Year brought some news. The bombing in our town had stopped, people started moving back to their homes, and the schools were to open again. As Constantine's truck was still making its routes, my father hired it to take him and me to town. The truck had escaped mobilization due to its wear and tear.

"For one thing, it has no brakes," one of the officers in the selection committee joked. "It would be like making a gift to the Italians if you were to take it to the front."

But my father said he would take his chances with Constantine, whose skills as the driver of such a wreck he admired. Besides, he said, he didn't want to walk in the mud.

CHAPTER 9

Defeat

Three war planes almost grazed the side of a mountain as they roared over our heads, flying southeast. A few minutes later, we heard bomb explosions, and a passerby said that the bombs had been dropped at the Bay of Nydri, a port used for transporting provisions to the front.

As soon as the three planes were out of sight, my father gave us the signal to get up. It was the third day of Easter, and he had taken us—two of my village cousins and me—to the end of the plateau, west of my grandfather's village, where a canyon started as a narrow gorge and ended up widening into a harbor at the western side of the island. He said if we walked far enough, two or three kilometers, we could catch a view of the ocean. But when the air raid interrupted our hike, we hurried back home. People had gathered near the coffee shops at the plateau center and stood outside. One of them shouted. "The Germans are attacking!"

"We'll lick them too!" another cried.

Women had come to their doors, crossing themselves and offering vows to the saints.

We left them chattering, but they too, like us, had realized that the reign of terror was coming.

When we got back to my grandfather's, we learned more details. Several cargo ships, loaded with provisions for the soldiers at the front, had been hit at the Bay of Nydri at the eastern side of the island, a few miles south of town. Later in the day, many people gathered at the village square, listening to radio broadcasts, and we heard that the Germans had already broken the Metaxas Line, and their tanks were rolling down fast, crossing the Thessalian plain. They were expected to reach Athens in a day or two. The Greek army, surrounded on all sides, had scattered.

We sat down to a gloomy dinner, interrupted only by the groans of the elderly folks and an occasional sob from my mother. We had spent Easter Day at Grandfather's house, and we were still there, as Easter lasted three days. Grandfather had killed the fattened kid from the goat I had taken to pasture (and fed it when I couldn't), and we had all shared the delicious meals. Grandfather had gone down to his basement and brought another bottle of his good wine; that lightened our mood, but we also felt the tension rising.

"Christ has risen!" we all said and then sang the Easter anthem together.

In the morning, my father shut himself and Grandfather in one of his rooms for about half an hour. When they exited, my father's eyes showed resolution. He had heard that one or two of the loaded cargo ships had not sunk and that people were rushing there to buy whatever foodstuffs they could carry. I knew him as a man of action, who didn't let circumstances defeat him easily.

He explained to all of us that he had a plan. As he still had cash in his hands, he thought of going to Nydri with Uncle George and one other person, taking Grandfather's horse and perhaps one more animal, if he could find it, and spending his Greek money, which still was good, to buy as many provisions as he could. Grandfather joined him, offering any cash in hand, so they could share the provisions.

They expected that the Occupation by the Germans or Italians would soon be here—and it would last.

"The horse could carry quite a bit," Uncle George observed, "but it might help if we got another animal."

"Right," said Grandfather, who rarely agreed with his son. George offered to ask Vasilis, He went out to find him, and both appeared a few minutes later. Vasilis was driving his father's donkey.

"Three men and two animals," my father said.

"I can carry stuff on my shoulders," Vasilis said, "if I have to."

That settled it, and the small group prepared to leave—but then an idea came to me.

"Can I come along, Father?" I asked.

"No, no!" my mother cried. "You are too young to go into such danger!"

"Why not?" my father said. "We will just go through the valleys, and the folks here know the paths. It will be a good experience for him. Besides, he has grown a lot in the last few months. And his shoulder is healed."

They all stared at me. I had grown, and my legs were used to treading the paths and climbing up and down hills. I felt proud that my father had chosen me to go with the group. I was anything but a daredevil, but my curiosity—honed as it was by my Verne readings—outweighed my caution.

I put on my jacket and joined the group but not before my mother hugged me. Sobbing lightly, she told me to be careful.

"I will, Mother," I said, trying to reassure her.

My father was not a rider and preferred to walk, so Uncle George rode his horse. Vasilis helped me climb on his donkey and sit side saddle, making sure I was secure and as comfortable as possible. He was such a mild-mannered person, always ready to help anyone at a moment's notice, that he had gained the good opinion of folks in the neighborhood. He hadn't been drafted because his eyes were not focused, and he wouldn't have been able to shoot a rifle. Nonetheless, that did not prevent him from being a cooperative and willing handyman.

Uncle George knew the trails, as his father had taken him to Nydri nearly every July when the big religious festival took place there. We cut through a narrow passage, leaving behind two rocky heights, and entered a valley, an uninhabited stretch of wilderness, where nature reigned unrestricted.

It was late April, and everything was in bloom. I was used to seeing terraced vineyards around the villages, so I was unprepared for what unfolded before my eyes. I could see myrtle shrubs everywhere. Spiked broom cascaded down the hillocks, spreading a sea of yellow. The climbing jasmine suffocated the few oak saplings and filled the air with aromas. And the trilling of warblers was a symphony of song I had never heard before. Gold finches crossed the air, trilling as they flew; a robin shot up like a vertical arrow; and larks, hidden from view, added to the general symphony. And then I heard a melodious shriek, outdoing all others, like a brass instrument in an orchestra.

"It's a partridge," my father said. "You can only see or hear them in the wilderness."

"Why?" I asked.

"They are hunted because of their delicious meat. They will disappear completely one day."

We walked another kilometer or two in the lush vegetation and then came upon a cluster of small buildings and a red church that sat on a height, surrounded by a wall of small rocks that looked like a fortification. A chant came to our ears, and I recognized the Easter hymn, "Christ Is Risen," which we ourselves had sung three days earlier.

"They are still celebrating Easter," my father said. "They probably don't know about the German attacks. They live completely isolated lives."

"What church is this?" I asked naively.

"Not a church; it's a monastery," my father replied. "It was built ages ago by monks who arrived from the mainland. It's called the Red Monastery, and in older times, it had extensive land possessions and large flocks of sheep, goats, and cattle. Those are bygone days, and now the few monks who remain live from the gardens around them and contributions from the worshippers who manage to get there through the brush."

As we passed by, we saw a monk digging a garden not too far from our path, and he cried, "Christ is risen!"

"Truly is risen," we echoed but went by without another word.

It was nearly noon when we finally reached Nydri. We had to descend a steep path, and the animals struggled a little, trying not to slip on the gravelly ground. I jumped off the saddle and went on foot the rest of the way, not wanting the beast that carried me to be hurt.

When we caught the first view of Nydri, I was dazzled by the beauty of the place. Nydri was built at the narrow entrance of the Bay, which widened, forming a big salt-water lake, swerving to the left and reaching the other side at the bottom of a hillock, where the Church of Saint Sunday, a white dot from our distance, was built. Rows of oleander greeted our approach, and the pungent smell of the lemon tree flowers helped establish a good mood. The plain of Nydri, enclosed on three sides by mountaintops, was the mildest part of the island, weather-wise, as it avoided the bitter north winds that assailed the northern parts. Citrus fruit was cultivated—lemons, oranges, and grapefruit—which were exported to town and across the land of Acarnania. The town prospered, and so did the villages in the surrounding areas. My father, a natural talker, told me most of this. He also added that this area was the place where Odysseus reigned, according to an archeologist named Wilhelm Dörpfeld, who had lived there and made his famous excavations. His tomb was across the bay, near the church, and visitors came from around the world to visit it.

As we came nearer, we witnessed the devastation the air raids brought to the cargo ships—two or three had been completely sunk, with only their masts showing, but the largest one was moored to the pier, almost unharmed. We saw a small crowd of people, mostly men with animals, negotiating with the captain/owner of the ship and some sailors from his crew. We could hear them bawling, some even coming to blows, while others loaded their animals and left.

Vasilis and I stayed back while my father and Uncle George walked to the dock, holding the animals. We didn't hear what they said, but we guessed from their gestures that they were bargaining—but calmly, as my father was a clever negotiator.

Vasilis and I went closer and helped them load several sacks, some big and heavy, others lighter, until the two animals almost sank under the weight.

We left the harbor immediately, only stopping to get some food at a local tavern, and started our return trip. It was around one o'clock, and my father wanted us to get back before the roads got dark. The animals could hardly move on the gravelly path uphill, carrying such heavy burdens, so each of the three men picked up a sack, to lighten their load. I offered to carry one too, and my father let me have one of smallest. I did that willingly, although I huffed and puffed going uphill. My father told us that the stuff he'd bought was mostly sugar, coffee, rice, flour, dry raisins, powdered milk, and dried biscuits. There were also some bars of chocolate, and he let me chew one as we climbed up the steep path.

When we got to the valley, our minds were no longer on nature's beauty, as they had been that morning, as we would have to struggle to reach our destination by nightfall. We spoke little and stopped occasionally to rest a bit, and the animals had a chance to graze on the surrounding bushes. But we had to press on, and I started to feel the effects of the long day's trip. My knees buckled, and I had to sit on a stone to rest, causing the others to stop too. Vasilis grabbed my bag so when we started again, I was lighter, but I still hardly was able to move. Vasilis was the sturdiest of the three men, so he placed his and my bags on his donkey, also the sturdier of the two animals, and urged me to climb up his shoulders, piggyback. I did so, and we went on another kilometer or so, reaching Grandfather's house as darkness was settling in.

As soon as my mother saw me, she hurried to give me some bean soup she had prepared and helped me to bed right after I ate. I sank into a deep coma-like steep and didn't get up until the middle of next morning.

CHAPTER 10

Occupation

The Italians arrived at the island in early May. They took over command of the town and key posts of the island, including all the harbors. Restrictions were imposed, such as a curfew at night, but the town's inhabitants were encouraged to return to their homes and businesses. A pall fell everywhere, as people saw these arrogant foreigners, who had been defeated at the front, occupy our land, while our proud, victorious soldiers returned wounded—many on crutches, sitting on church steps, selling their military coats for bread, or begging for alms, stripped of the dignity that victory had given them.

My father had choices to make, but he did not hesitate. He let his parents and my mother stay at the village, while he and I would return to town. I still had my final examinations to take before the summer break, and the Italian authorities allowed this to happen without incident. I was ready to return to the village, when, of all things, a letter from Uncle Stathis arrived. A friend of his, who had managed to get to town from Athens one or two days before the Italians took over, brought it to my father, he said in utter secrecy. It was a bulky letter, consisting of about twelve pages, written in Stathis's flowery handwriting, which I recognized.

My father took time to read it, and then he called Andrew and told him many details that I wasn't allowed to hear—Andrew, as usual, filled me in a day or two later on the most important facts. As it happened, Stathis had found a job at an Athens high school just before the Occupation, and he was likely to stay there, as schools would remain open. Chufas had returned to the front after being treated for frostbite, and he had been killed there. Stathis and Katia had reconnected and planned to get married as soon as they could. *Wow*, I thought, *the best guy gets the girl after all.* (I had read that in a novel.)

But there were other details in the letter that my father told both of us directly. We knew that Prime Minister Metaxas had died at the end of January, and his replacement, Alexandros Koryzis, had committed suicide on the day the Nazis entered Athens; so did Penelope Delta, a best-selling author of nationalistic and children's books and called the "Mother of the Soldier." My father added that the evzone guard on the Acropolis jumped to his death, and many other prominent citizens also took their own lives. The nation mourned, my father said, adding that no one could predict when or whether freedom would come again. The reign of terror we all feared had begun.

My father and I returned to the village on foot, cutting through winding paths to avoid the Italian soldiers who were establishing posts at key places around town. Once or twice, we heard them speak in their native tongue, which sounded a bit like the Latin I had learned at school. After a couple of kilometers, as we were gaining higher ground, we felt free to return to the paved road.

At the village, the folks were upset and fearful, and I saw that Grandfather had tears in his eyes. He muttered to himself and said he was ashamed to live to see our land occupied by our enemies. But his mood brightened somewhat after my father and I arrived, and he asked Father what we were going to do. My mother, who lived with my paternal grandparents at the old house, arrived a few moments later. She embraced me, crying to see me safe.

We sat around Grandfather's big table in his living room and had a discussion, my father taking the lead, as usual. He said he had to return to town and start his business again because the Italians said shops of all kinds should remain open; otherwise, they would lose their licenses and be fined. Everyone else, including me, should remain at the village, and he could send any food he could get by any means available. Constantine's truck would run for a while—the wily Constantine had hidden several cans of gasoline in his basement—so we could communicate with each other. My father insisted that we stay put until things settled and we knew how safe it was to travel back and forth to town. I asked if I could go with him, but he said no. He and Andrew could manage by themselves, as they could eat at Milios's, as long as he served food.

"One thing more," my father added, turning to Grandfather. "I think you should use the shelter we dug to hide valuable things—such as olive oil, for instance. I heard the Italians are going to raid parts of the island where farm products are grown; some people are already doing that. Let George dig holes around your yard and put things in."

"He'll bungle things up," Grandfather murmured in his son's presence.

"I'll be back in a week or so, and we can get things done together. Nobody else—at all—should know about these spots," my father insisted. "Better get these things done before it's too late."

With that, the conversation ended. We had a good dinner—Grandfather had killed one his roosters—and we went to bed with a bit of hope in our hearts. With my father at the helm, I felt safe, as did the whole group.

I stayed at the village until the end of May and through the better part of June. Father returned soon enough, and he and Uncle George spent hours digging holes in the ground, placing things—olive oil in cans, and almonds, raisins, etc.—in sealed boxes that my father made and then marking those spots with stones from nearby terraces. All this work was done at dusk or early morning so no one could see what they did. Grandfather came out and saw the spots, but no one else did, and I was told to stay away. I did, although I peered through some bushes and guessed the spots, approximately.

My father saw me and said something like, "Curiosity killed the cat," and "The clever fox is caught by all four in the trap," and other such trivialities I'd heard before. I said something he didn't like, and he grabbed my ear and twisted it, a method of punishment my teachers used in grade school, which I thought I had outgrown, as I had already turned fourteen.

My mother soothed me and took me directly to bed. She said, "You're turning into a rebel, and that isn't good for you."

It didn't take long before my father's fears were realized. One day, around the second week of June, an Italian truck stopped outside Grandfather's gate, and a small group of Italian soldiers entered the yard. They stood in front of the small landing on top of the outside stairs and saluted militarily. Grandfather, Grandmother, and I were standing there. My mother had gone out with Uncle George and a group of hired women, as it was harvesting time, and every hand in the field was needed.

An Italian officer spoke in Italian, explaining something, and repeating the word, "Vino, vino." I understood the word, as I was studying Italian with a dictionary, having been told the language would be taught when we returned to school. The Italians were asking Grandfather if he could sell them some wine. Willy-nilly, he came down the stairs and took them to his basement, where the big barrels were, took off the corks, and showed them the barrels were empty. He had sold his wines last year after the harvest, as he always had done.

The Italians were not convinced. They checked the small barrels and found that one of them contained rosé wine, which Grandfather kept as drinking wine for his household. The Italians cried, "*Bene, bene*!" They brought several large canisters out of their truck, pulled the cork from the barrel, and drained the wine until the barrel was empty.

Then they said, "*Gracia, gracia tante*," and the officer took a thick wad of banknotes from his pocket—I later learned they were called *per la Grecias*[3]—and handed them to Grandfather. Then they climbed on their truck and left.

Grandfather stood in the middle of his yard, looking at the money, transfixed. His hands shook, and Grandmother and I thought he was having a stroke. But he walked over to his fence, looked down on the cobblestones, and started ripping the notes to tiny bits. He did so for about five minutes, with his hands shaking, and tossed them to the wind until all were blown away.

Grandmother took him by the arm, and we all climbed upstairs to the kitchen, where she sat him down and made him some tea.

"Luckily, they didn't look behind his big barrels," she said, "where he hides his bottles of good wine. And we still have another barrel of drinking wine in the old house."

Still, the raid had frozen our hearts, for now we knew that no one was boss of his own house.

---

[3] This was the currency the Italians used first, before they were exchanged for *Isole Ionie*, which was exclusively used for the seven Ionian islands that Mussolini intended to annex.

CHAPTER 11

The Threshing Machine

Seasons come and seasons go. They do not know anything about war and peace. And when planted things ripen, farmers know the time has come to go out into the fields and do what is expected of them—harvesting their products that they had labored to plant or nourished to grow throughout winter and spring.

Grandfather had extensive olive groves, vineyards, fruit trees, and two large fields growing wheat, one just across the valley from his house. The wheat was planted in December, with the seeds remaining in the soil, covered in the snow. They did not burst into seedlings until late March or April. The young stalks were fertilized after a month or so, and in June, they ripened into golden ears of wheat, a marvel to the eyes, when they were caressed by the sun and waved in the breeze. Violent rainstorms and hail did, at times, ruin an entire harvest, and farmers prayed that heaven did not open its floodgates in April or May.

The year of the invasion, 1941, which was gloomy in many ways, was favored by the weather, and the wheat harvest looked bountiful. Grandfather was excited, and so was Uncle George, who had labored to sow the seeds last December. Harvesting began around the second week of June and lasted until the end of the month. The mowing was done by hired women, who used sickles to cut the stalks, and Uncle George, helped by one or two men, tied them in bales, which were carried to the threshing floor. I too helped by carrying water jugs to the mowing women, who labored hard under the hot sun. One of them was my mother, who volunteered for the work as a small repayment to her father's bounty to her family. I also sat with them under one of the chestnut trees to share their midday meal, consisting mostly of bread, olives, goat cheese, and salted sardines.

Early in July, as the threshing was about to begin, my father made his appearance. He had been absent for a while, and he had sent word that he had reopened his shop and that he had found new ways to make an income. One of those was the cut in his band saw rubber taken from the wheels of an abandoned army vehicle into thin slices, which then could be used as shoe soles. As leather became too expensive, he was able to sell them.

When we saw him, he was in Constantine's truck, which sputtered uphill and stopped in front of Grandfather's house. Helped by Constantine, he unloaded two wide boards, which he placed against a wall near the gate. They were about three feet wide and about a yard and a half long, bending and narrowing at the top, like flatboats ready to sail. Grandfather, Grandmother, and Uncle George all came down the stairs and looked at these odd objects with curiosity. I joined the group.

"There're threshing machines," my father explained. "You can save time and money by threshing wheat if you use them. Look!"

He pulled one of the machines toward him, and we saw that other side was filled with sharp blades, wedged on the bottom of the board, about two inches apart.

"These two straps are tethered to the saddle of a horse, which pulls the machine over the stalks of wheat, and the blades cut them to pieces. It's much faster than having a horse treading over the wheat stalks for hours."

Grandfather trusted his son-in-law greatly, but he cast a dubious eye over that contraption. I could see in his face that all this seemed too modern for him. He was set in his ways, especially in matters of farming, which he had practiced for his entire life.

But my father insisted. "Look," he said, addressing George, "let's try this just once and see what happens."

"Where did you get the blades?" asked George.

"Those are leftover pieces of bandsaw I had lying around, and I made good use of them," my father explained. "I saw those devices used in Thrace, when I was in the army during the First World War."

"That's seems all right with me," George said. "It doesn't hurt to try. But doesn't this thing require a person to stand on it and drive the horse?"

"Yes, a small person, preferably," my father said, and he cast a side glance at me.

The idea was put into practice in a couple of days, when threshing began. Grandfather had his own threshing floor just across the valley, not far from the wheat field, and the bales were already moved there. Grandfather did not go, as he rarely moved out of his gate anymore, but he did not raise any objections. He said his son-in-law was no fool, so he stayed home and waited.

One of the two threshing machines was brought there, tied securely on Grandfather's horse, which also was to pull it. It was a small white animal but strong and durable and served the family well. I had tried to ride it once, bareback, and it had tossed me off, so I knew it had a temper. I also knew I was not destined to be a rider.

All went well. My father showed Uncle George how to use the two straps, which were attached to the harness—they both hoped they would not break. The floor was already filled with stalks, waiting to be threshed. The usual procedure was to have a horse run on the stalks and crush them well, and then the winnowing would begin—to separate the chaff from the grain.

They said the new method would require that the horse draw the machine, which would slash the stalks to pieces.

Both men looked at me. A small crowd, including my mother, gathered around the threshing floor to see how the experiment would work. Word of the new machine had gotten around.

"You are small that we won't tire the horse," Uncle George explained.

My father also looked at me, but I could tell he would not force me.

I suddenly hated the whole idea—the threshing floor and the horse that had once thrown me off its back.

But I didn't say no. I clenched my teeth, took the reins, and gave them a little shake. The horse, knowing what to do, started trotting around the threshing floor.

All went well for the first two or three turns, but when the circle narrowed, I was almost thrown off by the centrifugal force. I learned to bend the opposite way, as a bicyclist does when he makes a turn.

Then, it all turned into a lot of fun. The horse trotted, and I held the reins and imagined I was Ben-Hur, driving his chariot against Messala. I had seen the movie.

This lasted about an hour and a half. Uncle George stopped the horse, and I stepped away from the machine, sunburned and sweating a bit. But by that time, everyone was looking at the result: the stalks of wheat had been crushed to little bits far more effectively than a horse trotting on them would have done.

"And it only took it an hour and a half!" said George, laughing and tossing his hat in the air enthusiastically. "It would take three hours for the horse trotting to do this—and not as well."

"Bravo!" the crowed enthusiastically applauded.

My mother took me in her arms and wiped off the sweat and the dust from my face. And my father gave me a hug and kissed me, which he rarely did.

His machine had performed a miracle, but I was in it too.

The threshing continued for a few days, and my grandmother found another boy, one of my village cousins, to spell me, so between the two of us, the job was done in less than a week—it usually took two weeks with the old method. My father rented the other machine to several farmers, who heard of the innovations and paid my father what they called a tithe—a small percentage of the grain, only 3 percent, but that amounted to several sacks of wheat.

But then, as soon as the threshing business was concluded, a festive activity in itself, an edict arrived from the Italian authorities in town that every farmer had to give 30 percent of his total produce to the city, which was now plunging into hunger. Civilian representatives would arrive at the village windmills, where the wheat was to be ground, and would take the exact measure of what was to be given. The fine for not complying would be the confiscation of a person's entire harvest.

My father came from town to confer with Grandfather on how the edict would be put into effect. Andrew came with him to see his mother, who was struggling to make ends meet. Since he was a baker, he had inside information on how the Italians intended to put their plan into practice.

"The Italians say that they would use the flour to produce small loaves of bread—*pagnottas*, they call them, as big as your fist—to distribute to the poor for free every morning, so the bakeries will be busy. How much of the flour the Italians will keep for themselves is something no one knows."

Grandfather stood silent, wondering what to do. He wanted to keep as much of his harvest as he could. My father guessed his thoughts.

"It's best to go along with the edict," he said. "You don't want your produce confiscated. If 30 percent is taken, will you have enough flour for the year?"

The harvest had been plentiful this season, Grandfather said, but he would still have to economize, if so many people were to be fed. He didn't quite say it that way, but I knew he had us in mind. With three or four people in the old house (us), he his resources would be strained.

"I wouldn't worry too much," said Andrew. "The *pagnottas* can't feed an entire town, so flour will have to come in from across the land, Acarnania. The folks there produce wheat and corn, and they raise cattle. And they are willing to trade in the black market. And it's already started."

"Wouldn't that be illegal?" Grandfather asked.

"This war is illegal," my father concluded. "And we didn't start it."

They stopped short of cheering for the black market, but Grandfather, as usual, brought out one of his best wines, and the feast that followed heartened out mood.

"And cheers for those who ride threshing machines," somebody said—I forget who.

PART II

The Traitor

CHAPTER 12

Massos

"The bastard is coming," Theodor said and spat on the wind-dried pavement. He was referring to a tall, blond man in his early thirties who was briskly trotting toward the school building. I had never seen him before, but I followed the example of Stephan and Panos, who were standing next to me, and delivered the Fascist salute.

Theodor turned toward the wall, raising the collar of his coat to shield his cigarette lighter from the wind. As soon as the man had gone in, he slipped the lighter back into his pocket; his cigarette, unlit, hung from his lips. "He won't last long," he said. "His days are numbered."

"Who's he?" I asked.

"Jerry Massos," Stephan informed me. "He's our new Ancient Greek and history teacher. He is pro-Italian."

As it turned out, I went to his history class that same afternoon and handed him a note from my father, explaining my first two absences were "due to the war conditions."

Massos smirked when he saw the note and silently motioned me to my seat.

"Greeks," he started out in a high-pitched, screeching voice, "have been a conquered nation for two-thirds of their entire history. First, the Pelasgians were overrun by the Dorians; Xerxes took Athens and burned it; then Alexander crushed the Greeks again; the Romans came and stayed for eight centuries; and the Turks occupied Greece for four more centuries! What does all that tell you? Is there an explanation for these historical facts? I'm asking you!" He had started out phrasing his words carefully but ended up bawling his questions at us.

The class seemed awestruck. Who would dare answer this overbearing teacher?

But a student in the last row raised his hand.

It was Stephan.

"Yes?" Massos leaned forward, his palms resting on the podium.

"What you said, Professor," Stephan stated, "is correct. But it is also correct to say that the Greeks always shook off the yoke of these oppressors."

"But that is hardly my point," Massos said, his ashen face reddening. "Hardly. My point is that Greeks were 'sponsored,' as it were, by these conquerors. They survived because the stronger nation—militarily and even in terms of a superior civilization—came in and took care of them. The Greeks suffer from incessant internal discord; in most cases, they are unable to rule themselves. In the old days, they invented a thing called democracy—I call it anarchy—and the result was chaos and endless bickering. Alexander saw this and united the Greeks by force, and through him, in a brief flash of brilliance, they conquered the world! The Romans brought another order and preserved the finer side of Greek civilization! Through them, Greek art and letters survived to be enjoyed by the rest of the world."

"How about the Turks?" Stephan asked. "Did they preserve the finer side of Greek civilization too?"

"The Turks provided shelter while the Byzantine and medieval world was breaking apart. Because of that shelter, Greece lived through the centuries. By itself, it would have become extinct."

"That's a distortion of history."

"Enough!" Massos bellowed. "When your opinion is needed, we will ask for it. Meanwhile, you listen. I am the authority here!"

During the afternoon break, Panos approached me as I walked in the yard. I was amazed by how tall he had grown, having gained a couple of inches on me. He was wearing a windbreaker, which revealed his slim waist and upper-body strength. His dress suggested to me that the war hadn't touched his family.

"How are things in the village?" he asked, casually enough, though I guessed what he had in mind. He knew I had been spending time at my grandfather's place since school had closed last May.

"Fine," I said evasively.

"Did you see Eleni?"

"Yes, a couple of times."

"And?"

"It seems her father is afraid of the Italians and won't send her back to school this semester."

"Did she tell you that?"

"No. She never talks to me."

"Then how do you know?"

"My grandmother told me. Eleni's father is her nephew."

Panos looked away, evidently not liking the news. "Will you help me elope with her?"

I was tired of hearing the same story of his elopement and the monks who would marry them. Still, I tried to sound sympathetic. "I would, if you tell me how I could do that."

"You have connections in the village. You'll be useful to us when the right time comes."

"Yes," I said, "but wait until we know how things turn out."

Stephan and Theodor walked in our direction. Stephan's face beamed, but Theodor looked sullen. He was a stocky, short-legged, red-haired fellow in his early twenties, far too old to be a schoolboy. I had learned from Stephan earlier that morning that Theodor had roots in the mainland and had come to our town to live with a relative. He told him that he was taking advantage of the "slowdown" in the war to finish his education.

"Did you hear that bastard smear our nation?" Theodor said.

"He couldn't come up with an answer, so he shut me up."

"Fuckin' ass," Theodor muttered, throwing his cigarette butt on the sidewalk and crushing it with his heel.

I walked away, not wanting to get involved in their discussion. I already disliked Theodor for his crude manners, although I grudgingly admired Stephan's courage. Would I ever have the guts to stand up to that tyrant? That's what the new teacher was. For the first time, I felt ashamed of a Greek, especially a teacher.

I had another class with Massos that afternoon. It was in the classics, and this time, he was all business, spending the entire hour analyzing a passage from Thucydides. But my mind, unused to paying attention to anything, wandered. I had a hard time concentrating on anything a teacher said. I could think of nothing but Eleni, whom I had seen at the village on several occasions—I had lied to Panos. The country air had coarsened her skin, but how beautiful everything else about her was! Her hair—dark and wavy and, now, uncut—cascaded over her shoulders, accenting the loveliness of her face. Her lips were full, like ripe cherries, and her teeth—well, she had actually smiled at me once. Did she still love Panos, or could she like me a little too? What a mystery that girl was! I couldn't read her mind, but one time, when my grandmother and I were visiting at her father's, she asked me something about school, and I thought I saw tears in her eyes. I too wished she could have come back. She would have been sitting in the row across from me at this very moment, and my gaze would have rested on her hair and shoulders.

The bell rang, and class was dismissed. It was the last afternoon class for me, so I walked home. My mother, who had come from the village that morning to see how my father and I were doing, was still in the house. The job of cleaning up the house was too much for her, so she had decided to stay the night.

She was cooking dinner—a chicken, which she had brought from Grandfather's farm, and spaghetti with sauce. She mumbled words to herself, upset to discover a basket full of unwashed socks next to one of the beds. "This isn't a house," she declared indignantly. "It's a barnyard!"

Meanwhile, the food was cooking on the fire, and the house was filled with aromas. I sighed with pleasure as I sat back on the only long chair in our living room and plunged into a chapter of *The Harbor of Love*, a lewd romance I had bought at a street book sale. I thought I had outgrown the juvenile Verne adventures.

"Go to Mataphias's tavern, and get some wine for your father," my mother said, handing me an empty bottle and a few per la Grecias.

I didn't want to move, but I had no choice. My mother was distressed to see me reading trashy novels and often complained I didn't apply myself with the same zeal to my school subjects. Once, she snatched a magazine from my hands—it featured a girl in a bathing suit on the cover—and threw it into the fire. Since then, I was careful to hide magazines in various holes around the house and read them secretly. But my mother, schooled in my tricks, knew where to find them.

Mataphias's tavern was only a couple of blocks away, but the walk gave me a chance to get out of the house and escape my mother's watchful eye.

I charged the wine and kept the money, figuring my father wouldn't bother checking when he paid the weekly account at the tavern that Mataphias kept for us.

When I got back, my father and Andrew, who worked at a nearby bakery, were home, and my mother had already served them dinner. My father, covered with sawdust and looking worn out, hardly gave me a look. Andrew had brought two loaves of fresh-baked bread from the bakery and was eating noisily.

"How's trading?" my father asked him in his tired voice, although I thought he really didn't care to know. These days, Andrew sold flour on the black market and was making money. He carried with him a package of banknotes, which he meant to take upstairs and lock it in his trunk. This was inflated Italian money, he explained to my father, but it was good enough if you had large quantities of it.

"I'm supporting a widowed mother, still grieving for the loss of our Zois, and also caring for two unmarried sisters—and I'm to provide dowries for both of them. With the sweat of my brow."

"Who buys the flour?"

"The bakeries," Andrew responded nonchalantly. "I don't sell to individuals. That would be like gathering pennies from the sidewalk. You don't get rich that way."

My mother, disgusted with this youngster's cocky manners, told my father later that he should kick him out of the house. He wasn't paying any rent and bringing two loaves of bread a day wasn't payment enough for his room and board. But my father liked Andrew's company and said he'd keep him as a tenant for a while. He and my mother had a mild argument after Andrew had gone upstairs to his room, but I went to bed without hearing the rest of it.

When I took my coat off, I found in one of my pockets a thin strip of paper with three words scrawled on it: *Massos must die.*

CHAPTER 13

The Two Sisters

The next morning turned out to be drizzly as well as cold, though it was only mid-September. A sharp wind rippled the sea-lake, and dark clouds had gathered over the eastern mountains of Acarnania, blocking the sunlight. My father sneezed as he went out in the yard to load the donkey with provisions for the village. My mother followed him in silence, her face drained. It was clear that these frequent partings had begun to wear her down. I could see that she was on the verge of tears.

My father finished packing. He had placed a couple of sacks of flour on the donkey, tying them with a strong cord on one side of the saddle. That morning, he had paid Andrew for the flour, he said. Now, as he helped her onto the saddle, my mother couldn't contain her indignation.

"He's duping you!" She stressed the words as she touched the donkey's flank with the end of the rope.

My father squeezed her hand softly and then watched her disappear around the corner.

What a life, I thought, *to be able to see your wife only once a month, if that!*

I left my father muttering to himself. I picked up my books and was about to go out the door when Sphaelos, the fisherman from across the street, came in, holding four medium-sized mullet in a box.

"Tell your mother I brought some fish for her," he said and stopped short of going in, dirty and smelly as he was.

"She just left for the village," I said and blocked his entrance. I had disliked that man ever since he had proposed taking me to an adult movie at the local theater, not too long ago.

"Well, I have to leave the fish here then," he said, seeming determined to go in.

"Give it to me, *Sior* Angelos," my father said, stepping to the door, his hand already in his pocket. "How much do I owe you?"

"This is just for you and your family," Sphaelos said. "I don't take payments from friends."

But my father gave him a small roll of bills. It was inflated Italian money, hardly worth giving to anybody, but it would be enough for Sphaelos, who had an aging mother and a growing son, to buy vegetables and olive oil on the black market. These days, the fishermen, who were no longer licensed by the Italians, fished at night, illegally. Most of them were starving, like the rest of the folks in town.

When I reached school, the drizzle had stopped, which I thought was unlucky for me because my first class was a marching drill in the schoolyard, run by the new physical education teacher, Stamalos, or "Jackknife," as he came to be known because of his weird walk. On rainy days, these drills were canceled, and students were left to lounge around in the basement, talking about girls and exchanging dirty jokes. But this morning, the Jackknife had the class already lined up and doing exercises.

I fell in with the others and started moving my arms up and down, as directions came from him, but my mind had already flown off to the mountains, where I imagined Eleni would be at this moment.

Was she ever to come back? Wouldn't it be a good thing if Panos picked up another girl and forgot Eleni? That would only be typical of him. He was a girl-chaser and an egomaniac, and it was just a shame that a girl like Eleni—so pretty and so smart—had been foolish enough to fall for him. It was only justice that the war had separated them. This way, she would have time to forget him, and he to find another. Meanwhile (didn't that happen in *The Harbor of Love*?), I could be the lucky underdog. I'd bide my time and wait for my turn.

"Fall in, smart-ass," the Jackknife hollered at me, seeing I was out of step with the rest of the line when the squad made an about-face. This teacher, who had replaced the well-liked Stathis, was already known for his crude language. *Smart-ass* was his favorite expression, according to Theodor, who theorized that the instructor had said that because he was gay. "He admires your stub," he spat out as he marched next to me. "Watch out."

I said nothing, disliking Theodor's language more than the instructor's. In the next hour, we were back in class, but my mind remained unfocused all morning. I began to worry whether I would ever learn anything, and I wondered what excuses I would give to my father if I failed all my subjects. Six months in the village, away from any disciplined work, had made me a colossus of laziness. How I hated being back at school, forced to learn, and taking orders from people I didn't like! Where were those delicious, endless hours of freedom?

But the afternoon started on a brighter note. Eleni came back. I saw her enter the classroom for the first afternoon class—with Massos—and hand him a note from her father, no doubt saying, as mine had, that she had been absent due to war conditions. This time, though, Massos was all gallantry, impressed by this beauty's entrance into his classroom. With a smile ill-fitting his expressionless face, he recorded the excused absences in his class register.

Eleni, her eyes haughtily averted, sat in the front row of desks, which were placed at an angle across the room so that the girls faced the boys.

I tried to steal a glance from her, but she kept her eyes lowered during the entire class period. Panos sat still in the back row, his eyes burning. I knew he couldn't wait for the bell to ring, and I felt the stabbings of jealousy more so now than at any other time. Right then and there, I decided not to let him have his way with this girl. Eleni had given me suggestive looks when I'd seen her several times in the mountains, doing the chores of a shepherdess, and that meant I had a chance with her. Why concede victory to Panos? Couldn't I too win a girl if I had a mind to? Once again, I thought of Panos's visible advantages over me. Eleni had eyes and could see, couldn't she? But then again, why count myself out?

After classes, I headed for home. With my mother gone, the house looked bleak. The fish still lay uncleaned in the kitchen sink, and there was a note from my father, saying I had to clean it and take it to Milios, the chatty tavern owner, who would cook it for our supper—unless, of course, I would fry it myself.

I didn't feel like doing that, so I took it to Milios, my mind still on Eleni and her return. She had disappeared as soon as the bell had rung, and I was unable to follow her. But I knew where she stayed, and after dinner, when my father went back to the sawmill, I sneaked around that neighborhood—it was only a few blocks away—and tried to catch a glimpse of her through the window.

I finished cleaning the fish and was about to step out of the door on my way to Milios's, when I bumped against Panos on his way in.

"Where are you going?" he asked, a sour look on his face.

"To the tavern," I responded. "I have to take this fish to the cook."

"Did you see what happened to me?"

"I have no idea."

"Eleni didn't even stop to say hello to me! Can you imagine that? She just slipped out of class and ran away, like a fugitive from the law. I can't believe she actually avoided me after the things we went through together!"

"Maybe she was in a hurry."

"In a hurry?" Panos exploded. "Don't you realize we were just one step from getting married? She could have been my wife! She almost is!"

"I'm sorry," I said, "but I got to go. My father's orders."

"Listen," he said, a little more calmly. "How about you and me getting together after dinner."

"To do what?"

"We can go over to my house, and you can pick and choose any of those books. My dad got a new Verne volume in his library."

His offer was not so tempting, as I had made up my mind to do something different. Besides, as I said before, I wasn't so hot about the Verne books anymore and still was reading *The Harbor of Love*, which had opened my eyes in more ways than one.

"I'll let you know later," I said vaguely and ran off.

Milios fried the mullet and boiled some greens, and Andrew brought two loaves of bread, as usual. When my father came back from work around eight, all three of us walked over to the restaurant and sat down to dinner.

I noticed Andrew ate fast, gulping down his dinner in just a few minutes. Then he excused himself and leaped out the door as if a magnet had pulled him away.

I gave my father an inquisitive look, but he was tired and hungry, and he didn't respond.

"He has a girl next door," Milios volunteered, guessing my thought. He sat down with us and ate too, since he had only two other customers at the back of the tavern, and he had served them already. The war had ruined his business, but he kept his tavern open, "just for show," he used to say to my father.

"Her name is Aspasia," he continued, "and she lives just a few doors down."

"Thanasis's sister?" my father said, his interest reviving.

"Didn't you know?" Milios droned on. "They've been engaged for two months."

"Two months! Why, the son of a widow hasn't said a word to me!"

"It's a well-kept secret. Thanasis doesn't want people to know who works for him."

"I might as well have known who his partner was too," my father said, hardly expressing regret. "That's how he brings in those piles of cash. Somebody must have taught him to hustle on the black market."

"People've got to live," Milios said philosophically. "Today, we live or die. No two ways about it. You might as well get 'fatty catty' before the Italians nab you."

"Still, he should have told me," my father said, looking vexed. "He ate from the palm of my hand. His mother brought him to me with her dead husband's coat on, three sizes too large. That's all he had on his back. Now, he makes ten thousand a night, and he won't tell me."

"Everybody's got to live," Milios repeated.

He barely had finished his sentence when the door was banged open and three carabinieri barged in. They wore alpine hats, cocked to one side, with feathers attached to the top. Secretly, people made fun of them, calling them "feather-cocks."

But these men also wore heavy boots and carried guns.

"*Via, via*," they kept repeating, rounding up all four men in the tavern, including my father.

"Wait a minute!" Milios cried and tried to resist. "This is my business. You can't take me. I haven't done anything."

But a rifle butt hit him on the cheek, and his nose bled. He, my father, and two others were hustled away in handcuffs, while I looked on in terror. No one had touched me. I knew where Thanasis's house was and rushed straight there. I knocked on the door, and a young woman of about twenty-five or so opened it a crack. "Who is it?"

"Me. Philios, Master Fondas's son."

I gave my father's nickname, rather than his actual surname, because that's how most people in town knew him. This young woman was not Aspasia but her sister Adrianna. Both were sort of pretty and looked alike, but I knew the difference.

"What are you doing here at this hour?" she asked.

"My father has been arrested by the Italians. Somebody said that Andrew Belelis is here."

Adrianna looked thunderstruck. "Come in." She took me by the hand, as if to protect me, and led me to a sitting room, where I saw Andrew seated at a card table, smoking a cigarette. Aspasia sat across from him, and they were playing cards. I could see that Adrianna had just vacated the third seat.

"He says Mastro Fondas has been arrested," Adrianna announced, and I saw Andrew jump from his seat.

"Where, where?" he asked, shaking his hands and rushing to me.

"At Milios's," I said. "We were just finishing up our meal and talking when they came in and took everybody there."

"It was a setup," Andrew said, sweat already pouring down his face. "A squeal. It was a full moon last night when we came in with the boat, and somebody must have seen us. I got to tell Thanasis. Where is he?"

"He's in the butcher shop," Aspasia informed him. "No doubt, they're going for him."

"I'll run over there and see what's going on. Meanwhile"—he turned to me—"you stay here and wait for word from me." He rushed out before any of us had time to ask him another word.

I didn't want to spend the night alone in that empty house, so I agreed.

The girls lived alone, as their brothers, aside from Thanasis, were married and owned homes of their own. As for Thanasis, his business always took him somewhere, night or day, and that is how these young women had so much free time to pay attention to their admirers—this was according to Milios, from whom I had heard more gossip than became my age. Both young women dressed somewhat showily but were well mannered and hospitable.

"Give Philios my bed," Aspasia said. "I'll sleep in Thanasis's room. I don't think he'll come back tonight."

I spent a miserable night, tossing and turning and worried to death about my father. Who would take care of me? What would happen when my mother heard about his arrest? Would he be released soon enough, or would the Italians keep him in jail permanently?

I didn't fall asleep for a long time and didn't get up until late. I hardly touched the nice breakfast of coffee and rolls the two kind young ladies prepared for me before I rushed to my house, only a few blocks away. To my astonishment, I found Andrew there. He had spent the night in the house, and now he was eating his breakfast as if nothing had happened.

"Listen," he said calmly, after I told him how miserable I'd been all night, "no need to worry. I've been to see your father. A friend of mine told Thanasis the Italians hadn't come for me—or for your father, for that matter."

"No? Then why did they arrest him?"

"It was all a mistake. The Italians had come for Milios! The stupid fellow had gossiped about an Italian officer who was seeing a Greek girl, and what he said was considered as slander against the Italian state."

"How about my father? When will he be released?"

Andrew spread some marmalade—where had he obtained such an expensive item?—on a piece of toasted bread. "In a couple of days. Don't worry."

"Why are they keeping him so long if they know he's innocent?"

"They said they have to go through with a proper investigation. Idiots." He finished his toast and put his coat on before leaving the house. "Don't worry, pal," he said, seeing my gloomy face before going out of the door. "I'll take your father's lunch to the jail. The carabinieri said I could. I have *permesso*," he added, proud of his Italian.

He went out with a laugh.

CHAPTER 14

Jail

I stayed at Thanasis's the whole time my father was in jail. The girls asked me to spend my nights there, and I couldn't say I didn't enjoy their company. They knew I was worried and tried hard to relieve my anxiety. They cooked tasty, plentiful meals, washed my socks and shirts, took me to the door when I left for school in the morning, and gave me a hug when I came home at night. In short, they did everything they could to please me. They even paid me compliments about my looks and manners.

Aspasia said I was growing up to be a handsome young man, and Adrianna commented that she had never seen such a gentleman in her house before. All this was news to me. I had always thought my looks were average and my height stunted, when compared to Panos, who was tall. But Adrianna, to whom I confided a few of my thoughts, said that height wasn't everything in a man and that some Hollywood stars, like Tyrone Power and James Cagney, were short. What does height matter if a man possesses more intriguing qualities?

Chatting like that in the evenings restored my spirits and relieved my loneliness. Andrew showed up once or twice but didn't stay long. He took my father his meals, but he said the Italians wouldn't allow anyone else to go near the prisoners. I didn't send word to my mother, agreeing with Andrew that it was not a good idea to worry her for the time being.

Andrew and Thanasis, meanwhile, had a "big operation" going, I heard from the girls. Together, they were getting ready to smuggle sizable loads of flour and meat from Acarnania. They had a difficult job ahead of them, trying to avoid the Italian patrols, and stay out of sight of the squealers, who were paid by the Italians to help them catch smugglers. Andrew and Thanasis risked their lives to make money, and they had to be alert. For that reason, Andrew preferred to sleep in our house, knowing it was safer, as he told me. He was afraid that one of his coworkers at the bakery might be a snitch, but none of those fellows knew where he was sleeping.

I had no control over what he did, anyway; besides, I preferred the company of the two women, who, having no other male in the house, kept lavishing their attention on me. Adrianna seemed to have a crush on me, as she hugged me and kissed me on both my cheeks when I came back from school in the evening. I didn't mind those hugs, which made me feel cocksure and proud that a mature woman liked me at my young age. And *The Harbor of Lov*e, a book I was still reading, taught me that many things were possible between a man and a woman, no matter what their ages. It was the story of a college student who lived in an apartment owned by a widow, who had a daughter. The young man was first lured by the mother and slept with her. He slashed his wrists after the mother caught him making love to her daughter, but he was saved in time and eventually married the girl. There were lurid scenes in there that sent me into fits of fantasizing.

Things at school went on as usual, and I picked up some useful study habits under the influence of Adrianna, who urged me to stay away "from that trashy book" (she knew what I was reading) and concentrate on my studies. Her advice sounded like my mother's, but I didn't mind it coming from Adrianna, and I even found it sensible. I spent part of one of my evenings doing an algebra exercise, which helped me pass a test with a good grade the next day. That and certain other things that happened a little later helped build my self-confidence.

What bothered me during those few days, though, was Panos's mania in following me around. I couldn't shake him, no matter how many tricks I used, and finally, I had to stop to listen to him, knowing full well what he had in mind. As always, it was Eleni. She hadn't spoken a word to him since she'd come back to town. Imagine that!

He kept buzzing my ears with such nonsense, so I tried to figure out a way to get rid of him. Since my father's arrest and after I started living at Adrianna's and her sister's, my interest in Eleni had diminished. I even thought I was a fool to have ever taken an interest in her. With two grown-up women lavishing their attentions on me and saying I was handsome, who needed a snooty, cold-hearted, adolescent girl? To hell with her!

But for my own peace of mind, I offered to do what I could for Panos. Predictably, he begged me once again (as he had done many times before) to be his messenger.

"I doubt I can do that," I told him.

"But you know where she lives, and you have an advantage, being her cousin. You have a right to inquire about her health, haven't you?"

"Yes," I said—to get rid of him.

Eleni lived at Tasia's, one of my mother's distant cousins. Tasia was a widow who made a living by renting rooms, mainly to female high school students from the villages. My mother had sent me on errands to her on occasion, so I knew this lady. But with my mother absent and my father in jail, what excuse could I find to pay Tasia a visit?

Well, I could think of only one cheap excuse. Since Eleni was my classmate and a good student, I could say I needed help with my math exercises.

As I anticipated, Tasia, a cagey, gray-haired woman, could smell a rat a mile away.

"What do you want, Philios?" she asked. She knew quite well who I was, but she peered at me curiously, as she hadn't seen me for a while, and I had grown.

I told her why I had come, trying to sound truthful.

"You can come in," she said, "but I'll have to let your mother know about your visit tomorrow. And don't stay long. Eleni's parents don't want her to waste her time."

I said I'd be brief, and she moved aside to let me pass. Eleni's room was on the west side of the house, upstairs, so I had to go in through Tasia's parlor, exit from there, and scamper up to a balcony before I could knock on her door.

From her room, Eleni could not go out of the house without passing through Tasia's quarters. It was like double security, so to speak. Orders from her father, Tasia noted.

I knocked. After a minute or so, the bolt was moved from inside, the door opened a crack, and two almond-shaped, coal-black eyes peered at me.

"It's you. What do you want?"

I shivered, standing on the balcony, which was exposed to the frigid northern wind. "I have a message from Panos," I whispered, my courage leaving me.

"Come on in," she said, opening the door wide. She was wearing a long, woolen gown, probably hand-woven on the loom by her mother. It covered her entire body from neck to toe. In it, as in anything else, she was maddeningly beautiful.

I sat on a chair, numb from cold and shyness. I could see books and papers spread on a desk next to her bed and guessed she had been studying.

"I have a message from Panos," I said.

"What did Panos have to say?" she asked, keeping her eyes lowered, as she did during class. Since I'd entered her room, she had not glanced at me.

"He wonders why you haven't spoken to him. He says you were going to be married. Is that true?"

"It was a stupid idea. I never consented to it," she said, and her eyes flashed.

"He told me last spring, before the break, that you were to

elope—that you were going up to the mountains and would have the ceremony performed by a monk."

"He doesn't know what he is talking about."

"He said you were almost like man and wife."

"He's an idiot."

"Don't you love him?"

"None of your business!"

I got up to leave. This girl was too cold-blooded, too vixenish. I wondered why any man wanted to have anything to do with her.

"Where are you going?" she asked.

"I'm leaving. I have to go."

"Why? You just came."

"It seems there's nothing to say."

"Don't you want to get an answer for your friend? Didn't you come for that?"

So she had an answer, but she wanted to play with me first. What a creature! "Well, what is your answer?"

"Can I trust you, Philios?" She blinked her eyes with celestial innocence, and she took my hand. She pulled me slightly toward her, making room on the bed so I could sit next to her.

Mechanically, I sat down, but I dared not say anything.

"You want to know the real truth?"

I wore a puzzled expression.

"It's true that Panos and I were going to get married. He had arranged everything, and right after Christmas, we were going to go to a monastery in the mountains, as you said. Then, my father heard about it. How this happened, I can't imagine, but some relative of his in town must have told him I was seen with Panos. He flew into a rage. For two whole days, he shut me in his storeroom, and I had to sleep on sacks of onions. Every two hours, he came in and whipped my backside. I was almost beaten to death. Here—look, if you don't believe me."

To my utter amazement, she pulled up the end of the robe she was wearing, to a point where the back of her thigh and her hip were revealed. An ugly welt, twelve inches long, still not totally healed, had cut across the creamy skin of her left thigh and disfigured it. I looked on with the fascination of a mad doctor poking at his beautiful female patient.

"How come I never knew anything of this?" I asked, overwhelmed and barely able to breathe. "I could have helped you."

She let her robe down and pressed my hand with appreciation. "How could anybody help me with that monster? Ah, you don't know what a father I have! It's awful!"

She had tears in her eyes, which soon trickled down her cheeks, making her look sad, like a weeping Madonna. I always thought women's tears were faked (except in the case of my mother, who was such a sincere person that I could not imagine her able to fake any emotion), but in this case, I was moved.

"You should have told me nonetheless. I would have done something."

"Thanks," she responded gratefully and squeezed my hand again, "but that would have gotten you into trouble too. No, there was nothing to be done."

"How did he let you come to town, then?"

"I had to come back to school. I wanted to finish my education because without it, I am nothing. I'd be a peasant woman, like the rest of them. So I begged and begged, and finally he said yes—I think it was just to get rid of my constant griping. But he laid one condition on me: If he heard that I'd seen Panos even once—or any other boy, for that matter—he would come downtown the first thing in the morning and drag me back to the village to stay there for the rest of my life!"

That was a ghastly tale she'd told me. Now I saw that my own problems, whatever those might be, were nothing compared to hers. I was a male and, therefore, relatively free. I could find a million ways to cheat my father and mother, if I wanted to. In reality, I was free to do just about whatever I wanted, but not this poor girl. At that moment I understood what it meant to be a woman—to be born one—and I felt pity for her in my heart.

"So, you are determined not to see him?"

"How can I? My fate is sealed if I go back to that village. I'll grow up to be an idiot, and I'll know about it too!"

"Do you want me to help you see Panos?"

"You? How can you do it?"

"I don't know yet, but I'll find a way. There are ways to arrange a secret meeting and even a secret wedding. Leave things to me."

She seemed surprised to hear such talk from me and looked at me with curiosity. "Philios, do you mean you really want to help me? I've always been lousy to you, and I don't deserve your help. Besides, I don't want to get you into trouble."

"If I get into trouble, I can get out of it, while you can't. As for deserving my help—well, let's say you're my cousin, and Panos is my friend. Let's leave it at that."

I knew my reasons were phony, and no doubt she knew that too. I got up to go, and she took me to the door, offering to open it. I walked out with a swagger, as if I had just scaled a castle and saved a damsel from the claws of a monster.

That night I had only her on my mind. Nothing else mattered.

CHAPTER 15

Revelations

I tossed and turned on the mattress when I got back to Adrianna's, unable to sleep. The promise I had given Eleni to help her elope with Panos seemed rash when I thought about it.

On the other hand, I was excited I could play a big role in her life. Perhaps I was in love with her once more. Despite the ugly bruise on her thigh, the sight of her soft white skin had sent me into convulsions of fantasizing!

Yes, I must help her. It didn't matter that, in the process, I would be helping Panos too. In her eyes, I would be a hero; she would be eternally grateful—and what else did I want? Did anything else matter but her adoration, her secret admiration for me?

A plan was already forming in my mind. I could bribe Tasia, a starving woman who often depended on the charity of her relatives (hadn't my mother sent her loaves of bread and pies?), with food from my father's stores. Because of my mother's absence, I was handling everyday food supplies, using the olive oil from the large cans, which my father had stored under the stairs, to purchase what we needed. Sometimes, he himself took olive oil to exchange it for other items on the black market. No one, not even my father, knew exactly how much olive oil was left in the cans. The cupboard too was stuffed with loaves, which Andrew, feeling generous these days, kept bringing from the bakery. What if I brought a bottle of olive oil or a loaf of bread to Tasia and said my mother had sent them to her?

That way, I could take notes to Eleni from Panos or at least have access to her room whenever I wanted—and wouldn't that be cool?

Then, there was the larger question of helping them elope. Would I really try to get involved in something as risky as that? Common sense descended on me for a second, but then my mind, once more, galloped back to its fantasies. Why shouldn't I? This wouldn't be just an adventure; it would prove I was capable of grasping the magnitude of a complicated project. It would help me gain the self-respect I lacked.

An elopement wouldn't be as hard to manage as I first thought. I would leave the arrangements about the monastery and the monks to Panos, and I would concentrate on gaining Tasia's cooperation, as she was the main stumbling block to all these operations.

It was almost dawn when I finally fell asleep. When I awoke, I heard shouting coming from downstairs. It sounded like my father!

I dressed quickly and tumbled downstairs, as I thought I'd heard him asking for me.

It was him, to be sure. He was standing at the door, blurting out a speech, of sorts, to Adrianna, who had just gotten up and still was wearing her bedroom attire. A dark stubble covered my father's face; his hair was tangled; his clothes were greasy and smelled of urine. When he saw me, he grabbed my arm and dragged me along with him into the street. He seemed mad as hell. I left Thanasis's house without saying goodbye to those two wonderful ladies who had taken care of me for the past three days and nights. My father wasn't in the mood to thank them either.

As soon as we were inside our house, he twisted my arms behind my back, held me still, and started kicking my side, his legs flying in the air. I knew he had an explosive temper, that his nerves had been on edge since the war had started, and that when something provoked him, he could kill you—or deal as many blows as you could take. Although his kicks almost softened my backside to a pulp, I took them in silence.

Finally, his fury was spent, and then I knew I had a lecture coming. To be sure, he delivered one—and a lengthy one too. He reminded me that this was wartime, that we were under an occupation by a foreign army, that our country having been invaded and enslaved; and that I was a shameless ingrate who had gained almost the height (again, my height) of a man but not any sense of obligation or duty. Where was I last night? He had come out of jail about nine o'clock and had gone home. Andrew told him I was staying at Adrianna's. He had gone there but found out I was somewhere else. He waited at Adrianna's for an hour; then, exhausted, he had come back home to sleep, having not slept for three days and nights. The Italians had allowed Andrew to bring him food only once a day. He hadn't washed during all that time, and he had slept on the frozen floor, where the prisoners pissed and evacuated their bowels. He had suffered, while I played around. So, where was I?

I was forced to tell him the truth—or half of it. I said that one of my classmates, whom I did not identify, had begged me to do him a favor, which was only delivering a message to another classmate, something that had to do with our lessons. I thought it would do no harm to oblige a friend. That's all I said. This was as far as I could go without getting myself, Panos, and Eleni into trouble.

My tone sounded sincere enough, so my father seemed satisfied, though I could tell he didn't fully believe what I told him. But I knew he had something else on his mind.

"And don't you go back to those women. They are no good, and they should've stayed away from someone else's business. Taking you in to live with them! What did they do?"

"But they were very nice," I protested.

"They're whores!" my father exploded, grabbing me by the arm, once more threatening violence. "I don't want you near them. Ever again! You hear me?"

I nodded my consent, but I could not say a word. I swallowed hard, a knot forming in my throat. I had developed a special fondness for the two nice ladies who were so understanding and free thinking and who treated me like an adult, not a child, which I wasn't anymore. But my father, tormented by anxiety and fearing that every step I took would lead to a disaster, could not understand. I knew I must obey him, but he and I did not communicate.

He got busy changing his clothes, and I left for school after munching a couple of hard rolls that my mother had left in a basket in the pantry. They still had some flavor, but they were getting dry.

I was late arriving, and class was about to start. I barely had time to sit down before Massos entered, a frigid look on his face, a square-edged ruler in his hand. As usual, when this teacher entered, all students stood up and raised their right hands in a salute.

I was still preoccupied with what had happened at home and failed (or didn't want) to stand up. And when I finally did, I didn't raise my hand. Panos had placed a tiny folded note in front of my desk, and I was trying to decipher the writing on it.

Massos noticed my failure to salute him.

"Eh, you!" he called out. "Step forward."

I stood before him, frozen with terror, as I looked up and saw his steely eyes staring hard at me. Before I could catch my breath, he raised his hand and struck my face, twice. Instantly, my cheeks were in flames. But the pain was nothing compared to the humiliation I felt at being insulted like that in front of the class.

"Open your hands!"

I did, and he counted ten smacks with his ruler. Now, not only my cheeks but my hands were on fire.

"Recite the lesson!"

What lesson? With all the things I'd gone through last night and this morning, I had forgotten entirely what today's history lesson was. I turned and looked at Stephan in desperation. He was the one who always knew and always helped others. I saw a word forming on his lips—*Julian*.

This wasn't much, but enough of a clue to get me started. I remembered Massos talking about the Byzantine emperor, Julian the Apostate, just a day or two ago. Julian had tried to bring back the ancient gods but failed. Luckily, I had memorized a verse about him that I had seen in my book, only because it had struck me as unusual. After a few words to introduce the subject, I recited the very words Julian had received from the Oracle of Delphi, which condemned his attempt:

> Tell the King,
> Daedalus has fallen to the ground,
> Phoebus Apollo no longer has a temple,
> Nor a prophesying fountain,
> Nor a sorceress breathing steaming laurel leaves.
> And his babbling water has gone silent.[4]

You could hear a pin drop in the room, and the class almost broke into applause. Nobody expected me to have an answer, let alone the right one. As small as I was and vulnerable, I still had scored a victory against this vicious country-hater.

Massos looked at me with curiosity, a sardonic smile already forming on his face. "Sit down," he said, and entered something in his class register.

As I turned back to my seat, I saw Eleni looking at me, her eyes glowing.

During the break, I found myself in the company of Theodor and Stephan, who descended on me the moment the class was over.

"Eh, I congratulate you," Theodor said, patting me on the shoulder. "You stood up to the bastard, like a true Greek."

"Don't mention it," I said, resenting his touching me on the shoulder, as if he and I were buddies. I thanked Stephan sincerely for his help, without which I would have been at the mercy of Massos.

They separated, and Stephan walked with me to the part of the schoolyard that was usually deserted, under the falling leaves of a wide plane tree.

---

[4] Είπατε το βασιλεί, χαμαι πεσέ Δαιδαλος αυλά, ουκέτι Φοίβος έχει καλύβην, ου μάντιδα δαφνην, ου παγάν λαλέουσαν, απέσβετω και λάλον ύδωρ.

"Theodor is part of the resistance," he informed me, "and he and I are looking for new members. The movement would be impressed by your sharp mind."

It dawned on me that I was called to be part of a group operating underground and that the scrawled note I'd found in my pocket not long ago was from him.

"We can't just sit passively and let things happen," Stephan said. "We must know what's going on. More groups are forming all over the place."

He talked to me for about ten minutes—the duration of the break—and I refrained from giving him a direct answer. I needed to think about this one seriously. I had no desire to join, but Stephan's help made me ashamed to say no. He might think I was evasive or uncommitted.

"I'll think it over and let you know," I told him.

As we were going in, Theodor joined us.

"That man who hit you," he said, "is a goner." He moved his forefinger across his throat, winking at me, as I watched in astonishment.

Back in class, I heard Massos talk for fifty minutes, but later, I had no recollection whatsoever of what he said or did. I thought I was allowing myself carelessly to be overcommitted. I had promised Eleni to help her elope with Panos. Now, Stephan was asking me to join an underground organization to fight against an occupying army. The novels I had read about heroes winning wars and getting the girl had filled my mind with fantasies, but I had no desire to play hero. Another sweet glance from Eleni as class was being dismissed made my confusion even greater. I can't say I didn't enjoy it, though!

I didn't get to talk to Panos until the final morning class was out. He had probably avoided me on purpose while I was with Theodor and Stephan, having other things to say to me than what those two had. He came near me as soon as were out of the schoolyard.

"Congratulations," Panos said a little coldly, thinking, no doubt, that it was fitting to give me a compliment for my performance before Massos.

"Thank you," I said, just as unfeelingly, as I considered his compliment insincere.

"Did you talk to Eleni last night?" His cheeks were red, his nose ran, and the few scattered hairs of the stubble he had grown lately stood stiff. I had never seen his handsome face so messed up. No doubt he had noticed Eleni's admiring look at me after I had stood up to Massos, and he was jealous.

"Sure, I did," I said and marched on, letting him follow me like a dog. Before we got home, I narrated briefly what had transpired at Eleni's place last night. I also told him of my plans to help them.

I saw his face come to life. Before he went in his house, he assured me all his books were mine and asked me if I wanted anything else in return.

"Like what?" I asked.

But he paid no attention. He shook my hand and went inside his house, as his mother, who had peered through the kitchen window, had nodded to him to get inside so she could serve his lunch.

I went into my house too, thinking no one was there to welcome me, but when I opened the door, I saw, to my surprise, not only my father but Andrew, Aspasia, and Adrianna, all sitting around the table. Thanasis, a curly-haired man with a swollen face and bulbous nose, sat next to them. He looked sleepy, but his mood was cheerful. All of them seemed in a state of euphoria.

"Guess what?" my father said, his face glowing. How he had changed since this morning! He was wearing a clean shirt and his new suit of clothes, and he smelled of barber's perfume. He had been for a shave. "Your uncle Andrew, here, is engaged to marry Miss Stephanou. From now on, you can call her Aunt Aspasia. The engagement will be in a few days. We are all going to the village."

The women had brought covered dishes consisting of fried fish, vegetables, boiled potatoes, and feta cheese. Andrew had brought his usual two loaves of fresh-baked bread. My father uncorked a bottle, which he had carried home from Mataphias's. I started eating silently, still sour for the way he had treated me that morning. Besides, Massos's ruler had left marks on my hands, which my father noticed.

"What happened to your hands?"

"I got smacked by the professor for being late."

My father said nothing, perhaps feeling he had contributed a little to my low mood.

"You can call me Auntie too," Adrianna purred. She sat next to me and leaned over to kiss me on the cheek, her knee pressing against mine.

They all laughed, trying to draw me to share their wineful mood, but I maintained my aloofness throughout that meal. So, there were two weddings intended for the near future: one organized openly and noisily; the other planned by me in secret. I felt those two events were somehow bound to collide.

And they didn't know they were talking to a revolutionary—because at that moment, I had decided I would join Stephan's gang.

"Look at the way he's smiling at you!" Aspasia said and gave me a kiss too.

"He's a sly one!"

They all guffawed.

That served me right. My father had brought the "whores" to our house.

CHAPTER 16

The Engagement

Andrew's engagement took place two weeks later, on a Sunday, in the village. My father and I traveled on foot, joining my mother and my two sets of grandparents there. Andrew came along with his future bride, as well as Thanasis, his two brothers, their families, and several of their friends. The engagement took place at a church on a bare hill, a hundred yards to the north of the village. The wind whistled razor-sharp, nipping noses and ears and numbing fingers. I sniffled all morning, catching cold, while the tedious church service dragged on, more a nuisance than a ceremony. Thankfully, it was over by noon.

A dinner followed the service, but it was a plain affair, and only the closest relatives were invited. Aunt Agatha came, bundled in a black headcover, still mourning the loss of her young boy, Zois. She hardly lifted her head or said a word to anyone. I saw Eleni, who came with her parents, her brother, and her two younger sisters. All sat at the table across from me, but during the entire dinner, which lasted over two hours, I couldn't catch one single glance from her. She must have been terrified of her father, a grim individual with a swirling black mustache and the shoulders of an ox. Her brother,

Tassos, a surly teenager and lookalike of his father, cast me hostile looks, probably thinking I was fancying his sister.

My father decided to stay in the village for a couple of days longer and do some repairs to my grandfather's old house, where my mother and paternal grandparents still lived. My maternal grandfather let them stay there for free, and my mother felt obliged to work in his fields almost daily, and that secured provisions, legumes, vegetables, and other farm products. But the old house was in disrepair. Part of the roof had caved in, one of the windows was broken, and the floor was full of holes. A scrawny cat my mother had adopted was supposed to chase the rats, but she was too old or too lazy to do that, and the rats found the floor holes an easy entrance to the house at night. They chewed away at the few sacks of flour my mother had placed in a corner. Though bombs were no longer dropped on our town, my father thought it would be safer for the old folks and my mother to live there for a while. I had lived there too and had little taste for the wilderness, crags, desolation, and sheer monotony of village life, especially in the winter. Luckily for me, because I was a high school student, my father had to take me with him in town.

I wanted to get out of there as soon as possible and asked Andrew, who left for town with his entourage the same afternoon, to take me along. He did me a favor, assuring my father and mother that I would be well taken care of and properly fed. My mother didn't like the idea, but my father consented, not wanting me to miss more classes. He only took Andrew aside and whispered something in his ear, keeping his eyes fixed on me while he spoke.

So I went with them. Thanasis had hired the one bus that still operated in town. It produced clouds of diesel oil smoke, as it sputtered along the highway, but I enjoyed the ride, which added some spice to an otherwise gloomy day.

Naturally, now that we were related—even as distantly as we were—I was invited to stay at "Aunt Adrianna's" for the few days during my father's absence. I was given a good meal—the second good one I ate that day—and was pampered by being offered her bed. Thanasis was spending his nights in the house this time, and Aspasia's bed was unavailable. Adrianna slept on a couch downstairs.

In the morning, I was off to school after a nutritious breakfast and plenty of expressions of "honey" and "little nephew," plus a kiss from both women.

At noon, during the school break, Stephan reminded me about a meeting at Vardania, a swamp bordering the western part of town, set for that afternoon after school. There was a shack about half a mile off, used by fishermen to store their nets in the summer but now abandoned. One could find it if one followed the footpath along the bulrushes, Stephan explained to me. Everyone had to go there alone, he stressed, for security reasons. I told him I was going to attend. Since my father was not in town, I thought this was an opportunity for me to meet the other members of the group and familiarize myself with the proceedings. This could look good in their eyes—and maybe they could leave me alone after that. As for my father, how could he find out? Taking advantage of his absence, I planned to do certain other things that evening that I had mapped out in my mind.

When classes were out at about three thirty, I followed the path and found the shack without much difficulty. The weather had turned colder than yesterday; the razor-sharp wind swept across the canal, rippling the empty lagoons at the fish farm. I froze without my overcoat, which I had foolishly not taken along because I was ashamed of its frayed elbows and the fact it barely covered my thighs. Low clouds above the eastern mountains threatened rain.

The shack was crowded with people, some of whom I recognized. To my surprise I saw Chalimourdas, the tough-looking rustic fellow from Acarnania who had been in my class for the last couple of years and who had fast outgrown me. I used to wrestle with him in the sandlot, but I quit doing that when he got too big for me. Like other boys, I taunted him by mimicking his Acarnania accent, and he chased me around the block to catch me and box my ears. I always evaded him, though, by managing to outrun him. As if his presence alone wasn't enough, he had brought along a husky fellow in a discolored military fatigue jacket, whom he introduced as

"Comrade Alkis"—no doubt a false name. I also saw Pippis, a young violin player, son of a wealthy hardware store owner, who had come along with his sister, Poppy, a young woman who had graduated a couple of years ago. She had been a university student, but the war had brought her back to her hometown. Panos was there too, unshaved and looking absent-minded.

Comrade Alkis took over the meeting, outlining his message in as few words as possible.

"There will be dangerous missions ahead," he warned, "so we must all act with caution. Groups have formed all over this part of the country. The password is 'resistance.' You must pronounce the word twice to be recognized. I urge you to obey your group leader here for speedy success of our mission. We all must do our parts."

He pointed at Theodor, who then took over the meeting. "Comrade Alkis is visiting from the mainland, carrying instructions for an upcoming big job."

A big job? What was that? I saw a question in Panos's eyes too. He sat stiffly, from cold and despair. Eleni hadn't been in school again that morning.

"Have you seen her?" He asked.

"She was at Andrew's engagement"—her father was one of Andrew's cousins—"so she must be late this morning."

But, as always, he worried himself to death about her.

Theodor started again, but I wasn't listening. Whatever he said simply went through my ears. I knew now I had not the slightest interest in the resistance; the whole idea bored me to death. Of course, I hated the Italians, who had invaded our homeland after losing the war in Albania—hadn't Hitler come to Mussolini's rescue?—and I disliked Massos, who had brutally slapped me. But that was no reason for me to conspire against him or anybody. And the folks from Acarnania were strangers to me.

Alkis and Theodor took turns explaining that Massos was being paid by the Italians to head a counterspy operation, working with a network of collaborators and squealers.

"Boaters," the husky fellow said, "are arrested every night as they cross the canal to bring in food for their families. The Italians catch them, beat them up, and then send them to the military courts at Preveza, where they die in the dungeons. The Italians know where the smugglers are and raid them at night in their hiding places. That defeats the purpose of the resistance because what the smugglers bring in is not only food for the starving but also for the guerillas. And without food, there's no resistance." Then he concluded, "We'll take care of the squealers. You take care of your responsibility here."

"Massos will be iced," Theodor broke in. "If we let him go on, they'll think we're scared of the fuckin' ass."

"We'll leave the squealers to you people from the underground," Stephan cut in. "But Massos is our boy; we'll take care of him."

My head spun. I had come to this meeting with frivolous motives, expecting to sit around until it was over and then go home to the pleasant ladies who were waiting for me. Besides, the idea of killing Massos was outlandish. How could a band of inexperienced juveniles carry out such a dangerous mission? From a side glance I cast at Panos, I judged that he shared my misgivings. Panos was idealistic but only with words. He could never outgrow the pampering he had received from his parents, who worshipped him, and I could see he was destined to grow up to be a perpetual adolescent. All he wanted was to marry Eleni. That was it; life would make him a clone of his father—selling leather on the island or some other town. How could anyone expect him to have the nerves of steel needed to help design, plan, and execute an assassination? For that is what Theodor, Stephan, and the husky fellow had in mind.

Of course, I wasn't much different from Panos. I had been pampered too—*stunted* was more the word—by my parents, who would probably attempt to protect me from life's perils until I was gone to the army or married. But I considered myself smarter than Panos, having read all those books from his father's library (dirty or not) that he never read himself; he just gave them to me. Stathis—oh, how I missed him!—had molded me to be "encyclopedic" (his own word) and said that smart people are educated people. These fellows here sounded cagey, but they were full of themselves and thought they could plan a murder and execute a man. The only thing they achieved, however, was to show what a bunch of immature juveniles they were.

Of course, I kept these thoughts to myself. I sat and listened, and after the meeting was over, I walked briskly back, trying not to freeze in the cold wind.

Panos followed me like a dog, with agony on his face, but we didn't talk much. I only assured him—to get rid of him—that I'd keep an eye on Tasia's house, all night if I had to, trying to find out whether Eleni had come back. If she hadn't returned by tomorrow morning, I would ask Tasia. I told him I planned to take olive oil from my father's stores to bribe Tasia, and he volunteered to give me a roll of leather from his father's shop to bribe her as well. Leather was a valuable commodity, and he was sure Tasia could use it to repair her shoes.

That evening, I left Adrianna's house after dinner, saying I was going to a schoolmate's to study, not saying exactly what. Andrew was in the house, so the girls didn't pay too much attention to me; only Adrianna made me promise I wouldn't be late. She also informed me I was to sleep in her room again tonight.

I scouted around Tasia's, trying to determine whether Eleni was there. My feelings were mixed. Why was I helping Panos elope with her? Why did I show such concern for him when I loved that girl myself and now was certain she loved me, not him? Hadn't I seen her expression change yesterday at the engagement, betraying her ardent feelings for me? She didn't look at me, for fear of her brother and father, but I could read her face, couldn't I?

Yes, Eleni loved me. Finally, I knew my heart. My love for her was deep-rooted and real. This was the one woman I would love for the rest of my life. Eleni was a serious, intelligent, educated person; besides, she had unrivaled good looks. None of the cover girls I had seen in magazines could match her exquisite figure. What a being! How could she be the offspring of a boorish farmer like her father? It must be an upswing of nature, a miracle or something.

Dazed by these reflections, hardly able to tell where I was, I approached Tasia's house. I didn't dare knock on her door. What could I say? Wouldn't Tasia—no fool of any kind—catch on to my ruse quickly enough? All my designs of bribing her faded into thin air. Would I stoop to such paltry methods? My sentiments for Eleni had emboldened me, and now I was ready for heroic steps, not mean actions designed to deceive. After all, Tasia was a decent human being; why should she fall victim to my low designs?

I closed my eyes, and tears started falling on my cheeks when I saw the light in Eleni's window.

Well, that proved one thing: she was back from the village and would most likely be in class tomorrow. The news would relieve Panos's misery, for one thing, so he'd probably get off my back. But what about me? How would I make my newfound truths known to her? I felt the strong need to reveal my feelings to Eleni. I had to do so.

I climbed up Tasia's balcony, scrambling in the dark to get hold of the railings, which were wooden and half rotten. I managed to spring up to the balcony floor, though this was not in good repair either and it creaked audibly in the crisp, clear night.

I didn't knock on her door—how could I? Love me or not, she'd take me for a madman, and she'd probably scream.

But her shutters were open just a crack, enough for me to peep through.

She was sitting at her desk, studying, though I couldn't tell what. She was writing on a pad in her steady, self-assured, calm manner. Even doing such a trivial thing, she had the stature of a queen. What a girl!

She must have been tired from her trip back because she kept yawning. After a few minutes, she put her writing pad and books away, stood up, and started undressing. She took off her sweater, pulling it up with her fingertips over her head. Next, her skirt dropped to the floor, and I saw her in her slip.

Should I continue to watch? I was conscious of my dastardly act, but I couldn't budge from where I was standing. Would there be another opportunity like this in my entire lifetime? After all, what was wrong with watching a beautiful girl undress?

Hadn't she herself shown me her naked thigh just a night or two ago? The whole thing was an accident. I didn't plan it!

But I was horribly ashamed of these thoughts and knew I had no right to invade someone's privacy, so I wrenched myself away. Then, something else I saw stopped me!

She knelt on the floor before an icon of the Virgin Mary, which hung on the wall, and she began to pray.

Of course, I couldn't hear what she said as the window was closed, but I could almost read her lips. Her chaste posture gave me additional curiosity, mixed with a degree of self-loathing. Wasn't this supposed to be a man's or a woman's most inviolable, most private moment? And wasn't I a wretched coward to invade that privacy? Seeing her praying made me feel more ashamed than if I had seen her naked.

I tore myself away and scrambled down the balcony. As I took hold of one of the rotten wooden railings by mistake in the darkness, it gave way, and I fell on the hard pavement, landing on my left hip.

Uttering not a sound, I got up slowly and limped to Adrianna's, with tears of shame and pain running down my cheeks.

CHAPTER 17

The Fall

When I arrived back at Thanasis's, I found the door unlatched and everybody gone to bed. I slipped upstairs and went straight to Adrianna's room. In the dark, I dropped my clothes hastily and got under the covers. To my utter surprise, someone else was sleeping in the bed! Who could that be? Who else but Adrianna herself! She was the one who had given me her bed. Last night she had slept on the couch in the living room. Why hadn't she done the same tonight?

"Thanasis brought one of his friends," she whispered in a barely audible voice. "And Andrew is in the house. I couldn't sleep anywhere else. I hope you don't mind."

Mind? I was intrigued, fascinated. I assumed Andrew was in Aspasia's room, and that, of course, Thanasis knew about this. Thanasis must be sleeping in his own room downstairs, and his friend was on the couch in the living room—I missed seeing him in the darkness.

Well, that was a quite nice fix I was in! Two males out of the four in the house had girls sleeping with them. My ethereal mood, after I had just dreamed of angelic choirs and of Eleni as a heavenly, disembodied creature of beauty, vanished in a second, and there I was, pulsating with desire as I lay next to a naked woman's flesh. My feelings for Eleni were heart-oriented. For Adrianna, I had felt almost nothing until now, though I was conscious that she was a physically enticing woman. I had guessed right—she was attracted to me; otherwise, why call me "honey" and "little nephew" all the time?

But I couldn't think ahead. I simply resigned myself to my good fortune, for what else could these things be called? I had just seen the best-looking girl ever, the girl I loved, praying in her slip. Now, I was in the same bed with Adrianna, a beautiful woman in her own right. How old was she? I tried to figure out her age. Twenty-five, twenty-six, at the most. No matter. She and I couldn't really be all that far apart in age.

I was unable to suppress a moan of pain, as my hurting side stabbed me.

"What's the matter, honey?" Adrianna said, a little more audibly this time. "Are you in pain?"

"I am," I whined, as if a bullet had shot through my left hip.

"What's wrong?"

"I fell from Panos's stairs." This was a patent lie. Panos's doorway had no steps, but I assumed Adrianna had never been in his house. I had to find some excuse.

"Let me see." She got up and lit a candle on a nightstand. She was not completely naked but not fully dressed either. She had on a silk nightie—where could one obtain such a thing during a war?—that nearly exposed her good-sized breasts and only covered parts of her thighs.

I showed her the place on my upper hip, and to my astonishment, I saw a bruise on it as large as a dinner plate.

"My God, you're horribly hurt! How did this happen?"

"I told you I fell—"

"You are being naughty. Didn't I try to teach you to have some common sense?"

"Who are you, my mother?"

"In her absence, I should spank you."

I said nothing, feeling she was right.

"Is it very painful?" she asked.

"Only when I try to lie on it."

"I'm going downstairs to the kitchen and make a hot compress. Don't move your hip until I come back. Just lie on the other side."

"Isn't that man downstairs?"

She must have known what I meant, for she slipped a robe on that covered her from neck to toe. I lay there, hardly thinking, waiting. How could someone like me behave sensibly or with premeditation, if things happened in their own crazy momentum?

Adrianna was back after a few minutes. All she brought was a shredded piece of cloth, soaked in warmed-up rubbing alcohol. She applied it to the bruise.

"Hold it there," she said. "The pain should ease a bit."

Then she blew out the candle and came under the covers, invisibly having taken the robe off.

The pain eased, but I could not sleep. The bed was double but rather narrow for two people, and I felt her warm body almost touching mine. But if she had any salacious intentions, I never found out because in a minute or two, I heard her snoring lightly. The scent of rubbing-alcohol came to my nostrils, and it must have anaesthetized me into sleep.

Thanasis's friend stayed for breakfast. He was a coarse-looking individual of thirty-five or so, with square shoulders and bristly straight hair. He sat monolithically on his chair, eating with mechanical movements, as if feeding someone outside himself. I remembered I had seen him a couple of times at Thanasis's butcher shop.

He spoke only a few words during breakfast, and I guessed he must have been a fellow from the mainland because of his thick accent—a drawl and twisting of vowels that was characteristic of those people. No doubt he and Thanasis were partners in some sort of business deal. Later, I learned that his last name was Karandonis, but I heard everyone calling him Andonis. His eyes followed Adrianna as she moved around the room, sizing up her figure, from her buttocks to her calves. Adrianna seemed embarrassed, and her mood seemed a little down, something unusual for one so vivacious. What was going on? Had Thanasis found a bridegroom for his sister? It was obvious to me that she didn't fancy this man at all. And suddenly, I felt jealous—and annoyed. Why did women have to have brothers who pick out husbands for them? Why were such injustices inflicted upon females by their male relatives? Didn't these women have feelings of their own, and shouldn't they be consulted before decisions were made?

Andrew sat next to his fiancée, unshaven, yawning, his hair tousled, no doubt having spent a sleepless night. He stretched a couple of times and yawned again, quite oblivious to being indelicate in the presence of company.

"When's your dad coming to town?" Thanasis asked me as I was eating a hard-boiled egg, which Adrianna had just peeled for me. His face was bloated and sourly surprised to see me sitting at their breakfast table.

"I don't know, sir," I said, feeling intimidated, and I got up to leave for school.

"Does he have to stay here?" I heard him say to one of the sisters, as I was exiting the door.

I hurried away, having left my breakfast uneaten—and I'd forgotten to take my books. Tears were in my eyes, and for a moment, I missed my father and mother and my own home. Up to that moment, I had felt great, as the two women had lavished all their attention on me and had treated me with the utmost courtesy. Andrew, I didn't mind so much; the fellow was all wrapped up in his love affair and his deals, and, in any case, he was friendly enough. But it was evident that Thanasis disliked me. He must have guessed I'd slept in his sister's bed.

I arrived at school too early and felt uncomfortable, having not brought any books or pencils with me. Would I be in trouble with Massos? Would he find me negligent and punish me again? I had a few coins in my pocket and used them to buy a roll from Tsirambas, the itinerant peddler, who carried his wares on a flat basket that hung on straps around his neck.

As I munched the roll, I walked around the yard in the cold and thought of the insult I'd received. I figured that tonight, I would have to go back to my house, even if I had to sleep alone there and without a dinner. A thin rain began to fall, and I felt alone and wretched. My hip was aching, and my mind was gripped with anxiety.

I saw Panos coming, his face beaming—and I guessed the reason.

"Eleni's back," I told him apathetically to forestall his begging me for information.

"I just saw her coming in," he said excitedly, "but I haven't talked to her yet. By the way she looked at me, I know she wants to meet later."

I was no longer interested in him or in her. Since I'd left Adrianna's house, my chest had been filled with a new anxiety and a new pain. And this wasn't just a feeling. It was a burning, all-consuming, physical, and emotional turmoil. Since I had lain next to Adrianna last night—I recalled the near touch of her body—a new thrill had enveloped me. Loving someone like Eleni was only a childish whim, a cloudy feeling that could evaporate any moment. I had wanted a real woman all along, one who could cater to my emotional and physical needs. Now I was finding out—Adrianna was that woman!

I sat through my morning classes in a dream, totally oblivious to whatever the professors were saying. Massos had an amused look on his face as he stared at me a couple of times, obviously thinking I was a hopeless case. He flung a question at me, something about the valor of Leonidas and his three hundred. I mumbled a word or two, entirely without any meaning.

He remarked derisively, "You've sunk completely, young fellow." He cocked his eyebrows in mock pity. "I'm not going to pass you. No, feeling sorry for you has its limits."

He kept saying such things, but I had totally sealed off reality. I wouldn't have heard him if he had come near me and fired a gun.

During lunch break, I had nowhere to go. Panos vanished right after the bell rang, obviously having managed to corner Eleni somewhere out of sight. For a change, I saw Stephan without Theodor, and he seemed in a mood to talk. He came near me as I was about to buy another roll from Tsirambas.

"Here," he said, giving me half a slice of bread with some cheese on it. His mother, Mrs. Diapsas, a common-enough sight in the schoolyard, had just come in and brought him his lunch—sandwiches, dried nuts, and fruit; too much food.

I accepted the bread, and we walked side by side, drifting in the direction of Vardania. On cold days like this, a few fishermen were seen there, rebuilding wind-blown reed cages to catch mullet later in the season. Only one of these fellows was working in the distance and was too far away to hear what we were saying.

"Listen," Stephan said, keeping his voice low, "I know what that bastard is trying to do to you, but you mustn't let him ruin you. He's being paid by the Fascists, who are trying to destroy our youth's spirit. Be proud of yourself. You're a Greek. Our ancestors were glorious heroes who fought barbarism for centuries. Are we going to let them down?"

His bombastic language didn't impress me. "What do you mean?"

"Nothing except what I said. You have to pull yourself together."

"What do you know about me?"

Stephan looked a little puzzled, but he was not one to be at a loss for words. "I don't know much about you. You're too secretive, never letting anyone into your real thoughts. I don't want to know. I respect your privacy and your feelings. I'd like to help you, if I can."

"How?"

"I'm not sure. But I can tell you this much: don't let that man fail you in all three subjects. Study enough to pass. He can't fail you if you know the material."

That advice sounded sincere and made sense, but I wasn't quite in a mood to take sensible advice. Besides, it didn't seem possible that he'd dragged me all this way just to give me advice.

"What else do you want?" I asked.

"Me? Nothing."

"What did you and Theodor say yesterday about the big job?"

"What about it?"

"You don't expect any of us to believe you, do you?"

Stephan looked incensed all of a sudden. He seemed to have had enough of coddling me. "If you weren't so … infantile, you'd know that I was serious."

"It must be a joke. How can boys do such things?"

"There's an organization behind us."

"Then why do we have to do anything? Why doesn't the organization execute this man?"

"Don't use these words," Stephan pleaded, looking around him, alarmed. But there was nobody to be seen; even the fisherman in the distance was gone. "Nobody is asking anyone to do things like that. All you are asked to do is stay alert and help when the time comes."

"Help, how?"

"You will be informed."

"Look," I said, "who is this Theodor? What do you know about him?"

"Enough to trust him."

"That's not enough for me. And how about this 'Comrade Alkis'? What does *comrade* mean? Is he a Communist?"

"I can't discuss these things in the street."

"Well, tell me when you can. Until then, I don't want to have anything to do with this Theodor. He's conning you, if you ask me."

He did not say anything else; he sneezed and pulled up the ends of his raincoat collar.

The drizzle started again, and we both ran back, arriving breathless at the school. But I got there first, leaving him behind by twenty or thirty yards. I wanted to show him that though he might be smarter, I was faster. Everyone in the school knew that.

The afternoon classes went just as monotonously as that morning's, but I felt a little better after my conversation with Stephan. His needing me flattered me, and the snappy answers I gave him took away some of the ire that had been building inside me since that morning. I was still pissed, though, and was lousy to Panos, who had followed me to give me the news about him and Eleni. He had seen her; they were friends again; she loved him! He kept babbling in my ear as he followed me to my house.

At my doorstep, I turned and faced him. "Listen," I said, "you and your girlfriend can go to hell. I don't want to hear what you do with her. Leave me alone!"

Panos was stunned. He had always counted on my wanting his books so I would always be his lackey. My eyes must have been dark and given him a message, for after a few seconds of staring at me, he snapped his fingers in my direction. "Go fuck yourself," he said calmly and walked away.

CHAPTER 18

Love Is

I found the house as empty as a tomb and smelling of mustiness. The rain had started again, and I could hear the pattering of the drops on the roof tiles. I fumbled for a candle in the half darkness and lit it with matches I found in the kitchen. Then I looked around for some food in the basket where my mother kept her baked hard rolls. Some had been there, but the rats had reduced them to crumbs. I ate a spoonful of molasses I found in a jar—it had strings of mildew running through it, and I almost vomited! I had decided to go to bed without supper when a knock came on the door.

I opened it, and Adrianna rushed in from the rain before I could say a word. A shawl covered her head, and when she removed it, I saw that her eyes were swollen. How lovely she was!

"My darling!"

A moment later, she was sitting next to me on a couch and kissing me so hard that my lips bled. She took out her handkerchief and wiped the red spot. "Sorry, my darling." She half laughed and got up.

I was too stunned to respond.

"Listen," she said, looking as composed as if we had been lovers for months. "Thanasis is gone for several days. So is Andrew. Nobody's in the house except me and Aspasia. Come and stay with us tonight."

"I don't think I should. Your brother might come back."

"No, he won't. And if he does, I don't care. Besides, you need to have your supper." And she pulled me by the hand.

Of course, I didn't resist and followed her, not being able to tell whether she was my lover or my second mother. She behaved like both.

We reached her house in a few minutes—it was dark now—and Aspasia had already set the table, so we sat down to eat almost right away. As usual, they had plenty of food—meat stew, fried potatoes, cheese, and macaroni with sauce. There was also a bottle of wine, and they poured me some. I was starved and ate and drank without looking at either of them. They did not speak much, and I sensed they were still uncomfortable after what had happened this morning.

"Has Mr. Andonis gone with your brother?" I asked, not really wanting to know.

Adrianna made no response, and Aspasia only sighed. "Don't say anything to anybody about him, honey," she cautioned me in her pleasant, soft voice. She was blushing, and then I discovered how pretty this girl was too. I again tried to guess their ages; they weren't twins, but they couldn't have been more than a year apart. At times, they looked older than twenty-five, closer to thirty. But now, both looked about twenty or even nineteen.

They ate little and fidgeted as they cleared the table and put away the dishes. I knew they played cards often, but most of the time, Andrew was their partner. Maybe they could play with me.

I asked, and they set up the card table. We all started playing Kontsina, one of the simplest card games, which I had learned from some of the boys in the village.

I figured out that probably this was the night that Thanasis brought his meat in from across the country. He and the fellow who was here this morning must have struck a deal, and they were carrying it out tonight. Andrew must have gone with them to smuggle his flour, or help them, or both. Such an operation, as always, had dangers, and that must be the reason why the two women seemed nervous. Or maybe something else happened.

"I'm going to bed," Aspasia said after a few minutes, putting her cards aside and getting up. "See you fellows in the morning."

I got up too, not knowing where Adrianna meant me to sleep. I waited for her to bring the mattress downstairs, the one they had used last night for their guest and had placed on the fold-out couch for better support. Of course, Andonis had been an unusual guest, while I was becoming a member of the household. No need to give me special treats.

Those thoughts were crossing my mind as I stood in the middle of the floor, not knowing what to do.

"Come upstairs," she said simply, giving me her hand. "You don't want to sleep down here and catch cold. I have a responsibility to your mother."

She said that calmly, not exhibiting any of that wild passion as when she was kissing me just an hour or so ago. What was I to make of her? My own feelings weren't clear to me either. I thought I loved her, but now I wondered. Who was she? A mother figure, just a friend and relative, or a hot and lustful she-goat trying to seduce an underage boy? Suddenly, I was afraid of her, but I could not resist following her.

She left me alone in her room, and I slipped under the covers quickly enough, not making any fuss. My day had been full of emotional swings, and I found that sometimes it was better to go along with the flow of things, out of sheer momentum, even if I didn't know the reason. Why not sleep off all this confusion? Better to leave unanswered questions for tomorrow.

I was almost fast asleep when I heard her come into the room. No, she wasn't coming to bed, it seemed to me. I heard her doing something and peeped from under the sheets. She was dragging the mattress out of the closet. She was going to sleep downstairs!

"Do you want me to help you?" I asked. I got up, and both of us picked up the heavy mattress, filled with lamb's wool, and carried it down the stairs. She placed it on the open couch, which was positioned next to the fireplace, and then put a pillow, blankets, and even an overcoat over it.

"Why are you sleeping here?" I asked, unable to hold back my curiosity.

"I'm not. This is just in case one of those boys comes home. I don't want them to disturb us."

"But you said they are not coming back tonight."

"That's what they told me, but one never knows," she said, sighing. "You just don't know. They're in harm's way. Anything is possible."

All of a sudden, she seemed terribly upset and broke into tears as she sat on the mattress. Her sobbing was stifled, but her emotion was just as violent as her kissing me a little while ago. She bit her lips, tore at her cheeks, even screamed, but in a muffled way, trying not to disturb her sister upstairs. I was too surprised to say anything and stood speechless next to her.

Finally, her sobs subsided, and she got up. "Let's go upstairs," she said.

I followed her, and we both entered her room. She made me sit on her bed, and she wiped her nose and eyes, looking sideways into a huge mirror hanging above a dresser made of dark, expensive wood.

"Why is your brother doing this dangerous work? Is it for money?"

"What else? He's never made money before in his life. How can a butcher do that? And now that he's found his opportunity on the black market, he's going in for a killing."

"But how is one to get rich with inflated money?"

"Thanasis gets gold for his trades."

I had heard before—that money that had come into the country from the British, who were organizing the underground and had circulated gold pounds. I knew these facts from the discussions between my father and Andrew while we were still eating at Milios's.

"That's how you get rich," Adrianna added philosophically. "My brother is smart. He knows what he is doing. Look." She opened one of the drawers of that dresser and took out a jewelry box. She opened it with a key that hung from a chain around her neck. "See?" she said.

There were three rows of gold coins inside, stacked side by side.

I had seen gold coins before—my father had about half a dozen in a drawer—but not in such quantity. I was impressed.

"That's all mine," she said, locking the box again and putting it back into the drawer.

I didn't have a thing to say to her, but I respected her immense (from my standpoint) wealth.

"There are a hundred pounds in there" she said, guessing what I was thinking. "A hundred more, and that will be enough for my dowry."

"Are you getting married to Andonis?"

Where did I find the courage to ask such a question? But this exhibition of wealth had made me feel a little jealous and increased my distaste for her family. Adrianna noticed the frown on my face.

"Well, for a young boy your age, you have decided ideas on who does what. I oughtn't to have shown you those things. I thought you were an understanding friend."

"So did I."

She looked at me curiously. "I'm not a crazy person," she said, and tears came to her eyes. "I'm quite aware that your father and mother entrusted you to my care."

"You have taken good care of me."

"No, I have not!"

She was again tense and nervous, fidgeting before a mirror, holding her hair back in a knot, and then pretending to comb it. When she opened her drawer, I saw packages of English cigarettes in it. Now she took one and lit it, exhaling smoke from her nostrils.

"Why do you worry so much about what my father and mother will think of you?" I asked.

"If they ever knew you'd slept in my bed, they would crucify me. And Thanasis told me before he left not to let you in here again. He said if he found you here, he'd kill me. And he is capable of doing that too."

"So that's why your sister was so tense? Then why did you let me back? I didn't ask to come."

"Honey, I can't explain. I'm terribly upset." She sat down and cried again for a good ten or twelve minutes.

I didn't know what to do. This was not a house in which to spend the night; things were getting too complicated. I was afraid that if I escaped Thanasis's anger, my father would give me a bashing—not to mention my mother's getting terribly upset! There was danger here. Thanasis and that other fellow might come back any minute now and bring back Andrew with them too, though I wasn't afraid of him. I got up to go.

"Don't go, Philios." She came near me and took my hand.

"Can't you and I take that money and elope?"

She laughed and squeezed me to her chest. "No, you and I can't elope."

"Why?"

"It's just impossible, honey. It can't be done."

"So, you'll marry that man?"

"I have to."

"Even if you don't want to?

"That's true."

"Can't your brother get you a decent-looking husband?"

"Thanasis is no man to change his mind about anything, once he has made it up. Andonis is his business partner. My marrying him is part of the deal."

"Are you really going to spend your life with that fellow?"

"It was decided this morning, after you left. They gave their word to each other and shook hands."

"Isn't that like selling cows?"

She seemed terribly offended by my senseless remark, but then she forced a smile again.

"I guess that's what I am to them."

"I am sorry I said that."

"That's okay, honey. You spoke your mind."

"Then, you are going to spend your life with a man you don't love."

"Yes and no."

I looked at this strange woman, astonished once more. She had twisted her hair into a knot, and her face looked fuller this way. She did not have Eleni's exquisite looks, but this was a woman who could think. Who knew what scheme she had in mind? And how did I figure into her schemes? I had no wish to be anybody's puppet. That's why I hated Stephan and Theodor and Panos. They had always thought of me as their errand boy. Maybe I was the errand boy for this woman too. But how would she use me?

"What do you mean?" I asked.

"I know I am a grown woman and shouldn't say such things, and you'll think me a harridan if I confide to you my inner thoughts, but you said you wanted an understanding friend. I have been that to you, and you can't deny that. I know you don't love your parents—for whatever reason—and I know your friends use you. I don't want to use you too. You are a smart, fine boy. You just need a little ... guidance. Then you'll do very well in school, and I predict that one day you'll be a lawyer or something. I truly admire you. You are just fine—and I wish you were five years older. Then you and I would have eloped—have no doubt that I would have done it then. But right now, such things are unthinkable. Where is an ignorant woman like me to go with a fifteen-year-old-boy?"

"I'll be sixteen soon."

"Honey, sixteen is no better than fifteen; for a man, it's even worse. Funny thing too."

"What is?"

"Your age. It's not wrong for being a lover—at sixteen, you can be as special as anybody, far better in fact."

"Have you had many other lovers?"

I thought she blushed.

"Some."

"Then they're right."

"Who is right?"

I thought of Milios, but I did not say his name. He and my father had gossiped about Adrianna's and Aspasia's being the "tarts" of the neighborhood. I never thought such comments had much merit. But now, it occurred to me that Adrianna's revelation proved their point perfectly. These women were what Milios said they were—took any lover who came along.

"I've had some boyfriends but not many. But I did have them, and that's why my brother abuses me frequently. That's one reason he wants me to get married in Acarnania, away from here, so that I won't continue to defile his name."

So that was it. Now I knew everything about her. Was that so bad? From my readings, I knew better. No, this woman and her sister were not bad at all. They had been repressed by their brothers, so what they were doing was a reaction against such repression. It was like me, rebelling again my father and mother, who still treated me as an infant, like somebody who never was meant to grow up. No, Adrianna was not bad, not like those women who go into the streets and sell their bodies for money. That was an entirely different thing.

"What are you thinking, honey?"

"I feel sorry for you."

"Why?"

"I just can't comprehend how you will live side by side with a man like … your future husband. Isn't dishonest if you don't love him?"

Instead of answering, she stuck the backs of her thumbs on the sides of her temples and wiggled her two forefingers. "In this town, they call these horns."

I was stunned by her abysmal cynicism. She seemed ashamed of it too and blushed quickly.

"Believe me, I'm not like that, honey. I'm not an evil woman. All I want is to be a little happy. But the thought of living over there, with the Vlachs, for the rest of my life, just isn't the thing I will ever, ever tolerate. Not only will I cheat but I'll kill him one day so I can get out of there!"

"I can't understand how one can *plan* to cheat a husband."

"I'm the one who's been cheated—of my share of happiness."

"Aspasia seems content with her choice."

"Bah! Her fiancé is a buffoon too. We're just been sold to these fellows. Like I said, it's part of the deal."

I found her explanation pat. This woman was bitter, but I still liked her. She was being honest with me—completely so, in fact—and I believed her. I liked her more for her honesty. This was a mature person who could stare life in the face and not flinch, unlike Eleni who, with all her good looks, was still a naive child. What a woman Adrianna was! She treated me frankly, but she also showed concern for me, my thoughts, my feelings, and my welfare. No other person had ever treated me in such a friendly, devoted, and honest manner. What did I not owe to her? How could I ever repay her?

But it was late, and all these fantastic revelations had really exhausted me, and I only wanted to sleep—and wished to leave her room.

"Can't I go sleep downstairs? I'm tired."

"Sure, honey."

I dragged myself downstairs, and got under the covers, trying to think of nothing but getting a good night's rest.

But five minutes later, shivering with cold next to a dead fire, I got up, and, as if drawn by a magnetic power, I went upstairs again. I did not knock on her door, just opened it. She was standing in front of her mirror in her nightie.

She did not say a word, and neither did I. But I momentarily stood next to her and looked at myself in the mirror. I saw no boy there but a grown man—someone I not seen before. Was it me or an image of myself?

But it was that image that went to bed with her. There were slight accommodations of weight distribution on that bed, but they didn't last long. I remained glued to her for a long time, and she didn't stop groaning: "My baby, my baby …"

I only spoke once to her throughout the rest of the night. "How old are you?"

"I am twenty-three," she said, kissing me, "for you."

I kissed her passionately too. I remembered some techniques I had read about in *The Harbor of Love* and applied them methodically. To her utter delight, I was a lot savvier in such matters than she had anticipated.

I thought of my father and of how he had instructed me once to stay away from "whores." He had spoken in the plural, but his remark had not been far off target. It was also he who had sent me to spend my nights with my new "aunts."

CHAPTER 19

Andonis Karandonis

Christmas came and went. School ended early, due to the reductions in the teaching staff, so I spent two months in my grandfather's village before I came back to town to finish off the first semester. I studied hard, and, with Stephan's help, I passed all three subjects—history, Ancient Greek, and Latin—taught by Massos, though my grades were low, to my father's displeasure. I gave him plenty of excuses, one being those prolonged school breaks. He had to agree that under war conditions, one shouldn't have too high expectations of a youngster.

Life at the village, nearly two months, hadn't been too inspiring, but I managed to live through it. Snow fell heavily a couple of times, filling our yard with white cotton candy, capping delicately the rows of firewood logs that my grandfather had placed over the stone fences in his yard. He had plenty of provisions of grains and olive oil, so our family hadn't wanted. But in town, hunger had begun to take a heavy toll. Most stores had closed, as staple items, like sugar, flour, or rice, had long disappeared from the shelves—thanks mostly to the Italians, who cleared the shelves, paying with inflated money. Only those who sold or bought on the black market could eat.

My father, who continued to live in town, visited the village every weekend, occasionally accompanied by Andrew, and both brought to us most dire reports. Our neighbors were dropping dead on their doorsteps, they said, and nothing could be done to help them. The Italians distributed *pagnottas*, one per person every day, but that was like having a slice of bread for breakfast, and that wouldn't fill a belly, not even a baby's; the little ones suffered the most. Hunger kills likes a bullet, but death from starvation is slower and more agonizing. One of my father's assistants, just to make some money to live on, used some planks in my father's shop to make caskets, which, for a while, became best-sellers (black market or not) because people had to be buried, once dead. Strange thing too because some people made money during the general starvation, being clever that way; as they say, "Necessity is the mother of invention."

The carabinieri, meanwhile, kept searching houses, going directly to hidden food supplies in wells and under stairs, looking for wheat or olive oil, which they then confiscated. They raided homes in the villages too. One afternoon, they stopped at my grandfather's, and this time they went for the spots where people dug and hid their products, for, as always, there were squealers who profited in various ways by getting word to the Italians on where to search.

Luckily, my father, as he had done earlier, had warned his father-in-law to move the things he had buried in various spots around his yard to his old house, where my mother and paternal grandparents lived. So the "feather-cocks" who searched his yard left empty-handed. Faking friendliness, Grandfather gave them some chickens (old hens, really) and a couple of dozen eggs, so they left, tipping their feathered caps and offering to pay, but Grandfather moved up his palms, as if greeting, saying, "*Niente, niente.*" He had now learned a lesson, for the first time in his life—to be sneaky. Still, a military truck loaded with foodstuffs was found in other people's yards, and some of the owners of these products were arrested. It was an appalling experience that left many villagers demoralized and indigent. Hunger spread in the villages, though the villagers could still eat what they planted in their backyards—radish, lettuce, sweet potatoes, and such. I saw my mother picking dandelions in the fields, like other women. She boiled them and served them with a few drops of olive oil, and we ate them with a piece of bread.

When I came back to town in January, my mother came too, to stay for a couple of weeks. The house was falling apart, she said, and she wanted to clean it and put things back in order. She stayed longer than she said she would initially, and by mid-February she was still there. My life acquired a new rhythm, which had its good sides, I had to admit. The house with her in it was no longer lonely; the place looked normal, the sheets were clean, and the floor was freshly swept every day. Good food cooked in the kitchen, despite the universal starvation outside. My father had traded lumber and services to people in the mainland, and piles of wheat and corn had filled our basement. These exchanges were legal, for the Italians hadn't stopped communications and didn't check the carloads arriving from the mainland—or were bribed, for they were hungry too. We, of course, did not eat meat and fish every day; my mother cooked mostly vegetables—potatoes, lentils, which were abundant, and other legumes. My father could afford a side of lamb occasionally or fish from our neighbor Sphaelos (whenever Sphaelos could catch it), and our cousins from the villages brought a chicken once in a while, in exchange for wheat or corn, which had now become a most valuable commodity. If you had bread, people said, your stomach could get filled; whatever else you put in there was secondary.

Thus, our family stayed free from hunger.

I had seen Eleni only a couple of times during my stay at the village, but she and I had exchanged not a word. When schools opened, her father, surprisingly, permitted her to come to town. He thought that she was already too educated and therefore was a bad influence on his younger daughters, who were still in grade school. In his eyes, an educated girl would refuse to do chores in the village—and then, how was work in the fields to be done? I learned some of these details from Panos, with whom I gradually reestablished relations. Of course, he was delighted things had turned out the way he wanted them. Seeing Eleni was the one thing that mattered to him. He still talked as if their marriage was soon to take place and said he was completing his arrangements with the monks; he would soon let me know about the date. To me, he sounded as much of a madman as he ever had, though I pretended to listen to him, just to keep him from buzzing my head with such nonsense.

I never went back to Adrianna's and had not seen her since that night, except once near the fountain at the square of Saint Paraskevi Church, where women went to draw water. She was filling a pitcher with water, holding it under the tap, and she kept her eyes away as I came near, pretending she hadn't seen me. I walked by without saying a word to her either. I felt a pang before I reached our house, a few minutes later, not sure whether it was of relief, shame, or sorrow. Probably all three.

My mother eyed me as I came in, her face purple. I had no idea what bothered her.

"What is this?" she said, shaking a soiled volume with a torn cover and a few leaves still uncut at the back. It was *The Harbor of Love*!

"Where did you find it?" I asked stupidly, unable to come up with a better question.

"Under the mattress!" she exploded. "Is this why your grades were so low?"

I said nothing else; I didn't even blush. It was always the same story—a woman, even though she was my mother, gave me lessons.

"Don't you have an answer?"

"Panos gave it to me," I lied.

"I know how you got it," she said in a softened voice. "Eat your supper and go upstairs."

I did so, but not before I witnessed the immolation of that wonderful romance. My father had brought lumber blocks from his workshop that afternoon, and I saw the pages of my beloved book ripped off, one by one, folded and lighted and fanning the flames of the blocks, until the last one turned to ash. I sighed and went to bed, intending to ask Panos if he would lend me a book called *Nana* by Emil Zola from his father's library. He said it was "much superior" to the one I was reading. I thought of the favors he would ask me in exchange.

The next morning, I asked my mother to prepare me a sandwich to take to school, not wanting to come back home for lunch; I remembered there was to be a meeting at Vardania that noon. She wrapped a piece of meat from last night's lamb dinner, some cheese, and a couple of slices of bread. She had tears in her eyes while doing this, and my conscience pricked me again for being so deceitful.

"Don't be late after school," she admonished me, and I promised I wouldn't.

After classes, I munched the sandwich on the way to Vardania, following Stephan at a distance. I'd been told that all the rest were to walk there separately, out of caution. The *carabinieri* were all over the place, as Theodor had warned me earlier that morning.

It was a windblown noon hour, and when I got to the shack, Comrade Alkis was already talking to the others. I only caught the tail end of his remarks. He was announcing something to the effect that our group ought to be ready for action soon. He didn't say much else, but Stephan soon filled in the details, as he and I walked back together.

"The order has been given," he said, and I could detect anxiety in his voice. "We should stand ready."

I was too astonished to say anything. How could anyone imagine that an enormous job like that could be handled by boys like us? For the first time, he seemed doubtful too.

"I know what you mean," he muttered. "But I guess what they have in mind for you and me are chores, like carrying messages. That is just as vital as anything."

I went straight home after classes, and my mother was pleased to see me. I spread my books on my desk and started studying hard, for the first time in a long time. I had passed Massos's classes last time, but it was with Stephan's help. This time, I would pass but with my own efforts. I did two algebra exercises, and then devoured a history chapter. I had started a passage in ancient Greek when I heard my mother's voice from downstairs.

"Philios!"

My father wasn't back from his shop yet, so she and I had supper alone. She had prepared lamb stew with the leftovers from last night but had made a special sauce and fried potatoes. She seasoned the vegetables with olive oil and served feta cheese. She had baked an apple pie for me, and I knew she had made a special effort to please me. We ate in silence, but I knew my efforts upstairs were appreciated. Maybe, in the long run, my mother could make a human being out of me.

A few days later, on a Saturday, after school classes were let out early, Panos and a couple of other boys from the neighborhood were standing outside the house of Yiannis Skepitsas, a local drunk who spent most of his time in the tavern. His house was abandoned, except for rats and cockroaches and a few birds that made nests under the roof eaves. Skepitsas had a mother and brother who had moved somewhere else to find food, and Skepitsas was more likely to be found sleeping near a sewer than in his bedroom. It was an old frame house with a brick foundation about six feet above the ground.

As we boys were standing near the place, talking of something or other, Nionios, the teenage son of Sior Angelos, noticed that one of the bricks was loose. He removed it and put his hand into the hole. To our utter surprise, when his hand came out, it was holding a sword!

Its scabbard ("sheath," Stephan called it later) had rusted on the outside, but a faded golden tassel decorated the handle.

We went around a fence, which hid us from the view of any passerby, and Panos unsheathed what looked like a magnificent artifact. The blade shone like a mirror, in which we could see the distorted images of our faces.

Who could have left such a thing in there?

"We must show it to Stephan," Panos opined, looking thoughtful. "This blade could be useful."

I considered that when this youngster's mind wasn't on Eleni, he could actually think.

"Or sell it on the black market," Nionios said. "It'll fetch at least twenty liters of olive oil, I bet."

But Panos disagreed. "Let's put it back where we found it. We're in a war. One never knows how things will turn out."

Nionios, a foul-mouthed urchin, cursed the Virgin and took the piece of bread that Panos had brought for him. Another youngster, Avantamos, from a starving family that lived near St. Paraskevi, also took a piece of bread and started munching it.

"You can't buy us with a couple of crumbs like that," Nionios said, emboldened after seeing Panos take an interest in the artifact.

"No," said Panos coolly. "Keep your mouths shut, and I'll bring you half a loaf each tonight."

Avantamos mumbled something and wiped his nose with his sleeve, but Panos silenced him with promise of more bread if he cooperated. Bread appealed to these ragamuffins more than an antique sword.

Then he put the sword back in the hole, blocking it again with a brick. When the others were gone, Panos thought I should take the sword and hide it in my house. He was afraid Nionios would go back, take it, and sell it.

"But I can't do that," I protested. "My mother is in the house now, and she'll see me."

"All right, then; we'll come back together tonight."

We walked back to our houses, saying nothing else. I was surprised to see Panos concentrating on a subject other than Eleni.

That night—it was now end of February—I couldn't go out, so I didn't keep my promise to meet Panos. My father had taken a rare break from his evening work and stayed home after dinner. As we were eating, Andrew, who still lived with us, announced that his wedding would take place next month. It was to be a double wedding, as his future wife's sister, Adrianna, was also getting married to a fellow from the mainland, whose name was Karandonis.

"Oh, Andonis Karandonis!" my father exclaimed. "I know the

fellow. He's one of my customers." He spoke these words with a jeering voice, twisting the vowels as he pronounced the man's name, imitating his accent. He always made good-natured jokes about the Vlachs—the shepherds across the land—whom he actually admired for their honest dealings. His sarcasm was put on, meant for Andrew, who sat across from me, eating his dinner.

I saw Andrew redden—but from pleasure, not from embarrassment—to hear his future brother-in-law being ridiculed in his presence.

"Say what you want; he's got *parades*," he blurted out, using a Turkish expression to indicate the Acarnanian's wealth. "Money's what counts in modern times. As for me"—he continued, despite a nasty look from my mother—"I came to this town wearing my dead father's jacket, three sizes too large. Well, I've been moving upward ever since, haven't I?"

"Who in his village could match that?" my father went on, winking to my mother, who was putting away the dishes and getting ready to go upstairs.

"Nobody in my village," Andrew bragged, "is up there with me." He pecked at his lapel with the handle of his fork as he spoke, to make his point.

"Give me that fork," my mother said. "And you"—she turned to me—"shove off to bed."

CHAPTER 20

The Party

Several dreary weeks passed, during which nothing much happened. Everything in our town came to a standstill, mostly because of the vicious winter. Snow fell not only on the mountains but on the nearby hills—it once covered the olive grove that stretched for about two kilometers west of town. The snow fell even in our schoolyard one morning; then, classes were dismissed, and everyone made snowballs, including the professors. Only Massos stayed upstairs. He had no friends on the faculty.

The Italian administration had appointed an Italian principal, whose name was Albanezi, and a teacher, Torri, who taught Italian. Torri was a tall, spindly-looking fellow with shy, tactful manners, saying only what was necessary, and we rather liked him. I heard that he had a reputation in Italy as a fine scholar but was forced by the authorities to travel abroad to teach to us. It had never occurred to me that these soldiers were probably here against their wills—forced to serve in the army, fight a war they didn't care for much, and now were occupying a foreign country. I stopped short of feeling sorry for them, since, willing or not, they had brought unimaginable suffering to our citizens, many of whom were dying of hunger in the streets. But I did try to learn Italian and studied hard. Stephan pointed out at a meeting that speaking Italian might come in handy during our planned operations. My studying Latin had helped me with learning Italian, as the alphabets were similar and some of the words too. *Patriam amamus dum spiramus* was one of my favorite Latin phrases, and I repeated it in its Greek equivalent: "We love our country as long as we breathe." I bragged to Stephan that I was becoming a linguist, but he was far ahead of me in both languages, and he just chuckled.

With all this going on, Andrew's wedding date was set for the last Sunday of March. The weather improved, as the wind had shifted to the south, bringing moisture for several days. When the snows melted, the sky became clear, and we all thought spring had set in. But just before the wedding day, the weather changed again. A north wind blew, the street pavement froze, and, once more, the skies threatened snowfall.

My mother left for the village a couple of days before the wedding. She disliked Andrew—she made no secret of that—and had always urged my father to kick the insolent youngster out of the house; why should he live at our expense? Andrew, aside from the two loaves of bread he brought every day, had never paid rent. Why should we be taken advantage of?

But my father, despite his occasional sarcasm aimed at Andrew, didn't have the heart to kick out the man who brought him his food while he was in jail. He gave his side of the argument, but my mother looked sore. She wasn't convinced, and she didn't want to be around to witness an event for which she had no taste. In any case, she also wanted to see how things were being run by my elderly grandparents in the village, and she had responsibilities there too. I agreed, realizing how strong she really was, having accomplished the difficult task of restraining my reckless habits. Hadn't I reformed during her brief stay in town? I had to admit this to myself as she kissed me goodbye. Vasilis had brought his donkey again, and she climbed up and sat on the saddle. "Be good," she said and touched my hand. Then she took off, leaving two desolate males alone again.

That Sunday, my father put on his clean shirt, and both of us went to the Church of St. Nicolas, where the wedding ceremony was to take place. I would have followed my mother to the village gladly, but, unlike her, I had no excuses that I could reveal. So, I stood next to my father, enduring the endless droning of Priest Spyridon as he performed the ceremony, which followed the regular Sunday services.

I felt grumpy and embarrassed. I knew Adrianna was marrying Andonis against her will—hadn't she told me that? I stole a couple of glances at her, and I saw her ashen expression under the bridal veil. Blood rushed to my cheeks, and I fantasized that I'd dash forward, push the crowd aside, grab her by the hand, and lead her away to live with me forever.

But in a moment, I put aside such reckless thoughts. Why should I feel sorry for her? Hadn't she cajoled me into her house and seduced me? Since my mother had given me several extensive lectures (could she have imagined what I did?), I had resisted doing things on an impulse. I saw now that I was all too prone to rush into emotional tangles, to act without thinking. Those things about damsels being rescued by heroes that I'd read in romances inflamed my imagination, at the expense of cool judgment. I could now see the dangers of these liaisons.

Though I grew stronger with these thoughts, I also felt emptier. True, I had risen above my weaknesses. I had taught myself to be level-headed and determined to tread on a straight path. But my life also had become dull and purposeless. What would I do without love? How much more exciting it was to think of a girl's face every minute of the day!

The end of the ceremony brought me back to reality. Most of the crowd in the church—friends, relatives, and other guests—were invited to the wedding party, which would consist of a reception at Thanasis's house first and then dinner at Milios's tavern. That arrangement, my father said, was made because Thanasis really meant to give a lavish dinner to his guests, and there was no way his house could accommodate all of them—not even half! So arrangements were made to rent the restaurant for the entire Sunday. Milios had been out of jail for several months and had reopened his tavern, which now attracted Italian soldiers—carabinieri were seen there frequently, drinking his wine and eating whatever food he could come up with. They paid him with "worthless paper," as everyone called their money.

Remembering his previous troubles, however, Milios kept mum, saying nothing about the obvious damage to his business, for fear of being sent to jail again. Some people speculated that the Italians had allowed him to trade secretly in exchange for bribes, and Milios was making a fortune. But he himself complained of the opposite, cursing those who spread such rumors. He was such a clown that no one believed him anymore.

Be that as it may, the restaurant was decorated with flowers, tables had been joined together for a better seating arrangement, and from the kitchen at the back came the aroma of roasting lamb, broiling fish, and stewed meat. Milios's two girls, his wife, and several female relatives from Thanasis's side of the family were assisting—setting the tables, spreading tablecloths, carrying bread and salads, and arranging chairs. The place was large enough to hold fifty or sixty guests. And there were that many—and more. The whole neighborhood, it seemed, smelled the food and poured in.

And why not? Everybody knew Thanasis had made money in the black market and that there would be plenty to eat. In the middle of severe hunger, a meal came to the people's stomachs—and it was free! And such a meal, most of them hadn't seen for a long time, perhaps not even in their entire lifetimes.

My father and I sat at a corner by ourselves. I recognized many of the people around me. There was Gus Sgouropoulos, a next-door neighbor, with his six children, all looking like deflated bedbugs. In came Mr. and Mrs. Mitsialis. He had been one of the most prosperous cloth merchants in our city in prewar days, parading the streets in his lofty trot and a watch with a gold chain decorating his substantial stomach. Now, he looked like a balloon with the air out. His cheeks were sunken, his watering left eye blinked, and his hands shook. His wife led him to a corner table, where both sat, and she started feeding him pieces of meat that she had cut carefully into tiny pieces. That's all she fed him during the entire dinner.

More neighbors came in, some lining up outside, like patrons at a cafeteria. *Sior* Angelos brought his ninety-year-old mother, an aged lady who drooled and mumbled; she was turning around and didn't seem to know where she was. She finally settled before a pile of chicken legs and started nibbling with her one tooth, her eyes twinkling with delight.

Nionios had grabbed a side of barbecued lamb ribs and sank his teeth into it. Avantamos was there with his mother and sister, filling their plates with salad, cheese, bread, meatballs, and fish. I saw Mrs. Stavrou, a widow who lived across the street from us. Her husband had died a few months ago; so had her teenage son—both from tuberculosis, people said. She was there with her daughter, Katina, a teenage girl who was as thin as a sheet.

Thanasis dropped in to make sure his guests were being served, and then he left; the brides and their grooms had disappeared right after the ceremony. Only some of the in-laws remained at the restaurant and, of course, Milios, with his wife and daughters. They worked hard, bringing in what looked like tons of food. Here came another roast lamb, several barbecued sides of beef, and a dozen platters of fish. There were loaves of bread, chunks of white cheese, two huge bowls of salad, and then, more fish, more beef, more chicken!

Neighbors poured in, sat down, and, without saying anything to anyone, began to eat. No one seemed eager to leave. Why should they? In the middle of a famine, this was an opportunity to eat, and eat they must. They would store as much food in their stomachs as they could, to fill them for as long as possible.

This theory, though, worked up to a certain point. Weakened from starvation, how much food could a stomach hold? Some turned away, looking sick, and left. But the majority remained where they were, bravely glancing at the plates being replenished. Jaws moved up and down with determination; teeth sank into chunks of meat; fingers cleaned bones.

The tables now looked like an abandoned battlefield, with piles of fish heads and picked chicken wings, scattered crumbs of bread, and spilled sauce all over the tablecloth. A suckling pig, now a skeleton of vertebrate, was replaced by a larger and juicier one. The guests, making a final effort, like soldiers on a battlefield, attacked the remaining dishes. But they weren't equal to the task. Could they eat all the food that was served? Much was still in front of them, like a mountain blocking a passage. The men loosened their belts; the women unbuckled their corsets. Hiccupping heavily, their eyes bulging from the strain, the guests ate on—and on. Milios again sprang into action; he and his wife and daughters brought in another side of beef, another leg of lamb, more chicken, more fish, more bread, more cheese. Undaunted, the guests ate on.

Any pretense that this was a wedding party was now dropped. It was more like a scene of cannibalism or like a jungle scene in which animals fall on a carcass. All went on in silence, except for the sound of chewing. No wine was consumed, no music was heard, no song—things so usual in Greek festivities. In this party, eating was all.

I didn't eat much. I tasted the roast lamb and picked a few potatoes from the platter, and that was all. I liked the peaches, though, which were placed in the corner of a table like a small pyramid, and I kept chewing them. My father found a dish to his liking, a small pot of stewed rabbit, and chewed on it for half an hour or so. But he wasn't a big eater; he soon gave up and told me it was time to go. We were about to do that when the door opened, and a group of carabinieri came in.

They didn't seem in a hostile mood; they apparently had come in only to eat. Milios rushed to them, cleared a table, sat them down, and ran into his kitchen to bring something fresh. It seemed a side of a roast pig had survived the voracity of his guests; there also were several sticks of salami, chicken stew, potatoes, and some spareribs. He spread these things before the Italians, who also asked for wine. Milios obliged them, and the carabinieri fell on the food, looking as hungry as the guests, most of whom continued to eat, ignoring the presence of the Italians. Soon, the dinner became a joint endeavor.

The Italians, who consumed wine in large quantities, soon got drunk. Several sprang to their feet, and one of them pulled a harmonica from his pocket and started a tune, which the guests recognized. It was "Hail to Mussolini" (which the Greeks had converted to "Suck It to Mussolini"). Now, the Greeks got up and, encouraged to sing too, started their own version of the song. The two versions got mixed up, but the Italians couldn't have cared less what was sung. Two of them danced the polka, one leading the other, while some of the Greeks, now drinking wine too, soon did the same. We heard "*Viva Duce*" coming from the Greeks, and "*Viva Grecias*" coming from the Italians. It was all drunken drollery and sheer madness. Who cared about the war anymore?

"Let's go," my father said, having had enough of that disorderly affair.

I followed him, glad to get away from the happenings of that hideous Sunday. I still recalled Adrianna's pale face under her veil and wondered where she was now. Where was Andonis taking her for their honeymoon? To his village? What a disaster for the poor woman. Even someone of Adrianna' s moral depravity didn't deserve such a fate.

It was cold outside and dark, and I stumbled while following my father, who always walked at a brisk trot. I couldn't quite catch up with him, so I lingered behind, gloomy at the thought of returning to an empty house. Andrew had moved out that morning, so here I was again, alone and cold, in that gaping hole!

My father had already gone inside, leaving the door open, and I was about to go in when Panos popped out of the darkness and grabbed me by the arm.

"I saw Stephan this afternoon," he whispered.

I shook his hand off. "And?"

"He said to tell you to pick up that sword and hide it. He's afraid those two"—he meant Nionios and Avantamos—"will steal it."

"I can do that after school tomorrow," I said, yawning. "Besides, those two just had big meals."

"We got to do it now. The sword won't be there tomorrow if we leave it."

"How in the world am I to do that? And where am I to hide it?"

"In your house. I know your mother is gone."

"But my father is inside."

"Come on; it won't take a moment. Besides, I got news."

Unable to resist, I followed him. My father had gone inside; he probably thought I was in the toilet in the yard.

After a few steps, Panos stopped. "Listen," he said, "you're right. The sword can wait until tomorrow. That's not the reason I waited for you."

"So what the shit do you want?" I said, irritated.

"Don't be so insensitive. Be my friend for a change."

There was emotion in his voice, and I was forced to listen.

"All right."

"I'm getting married next Sunday."

"Are you out of your mind?"

"Maybe. But that's a fact. Don't you want to help me?"

I said yes out of sheer annoyance.

"Also, Theodor wants us at a meeting tomorrow. The order was given."

"I don't want anything to do with that guy," I said. "He is a con man."

"But you gave me your word!"

"I gave no such word. I'm out of your silly schemes for good."

"And my marriage?" he whimpered.

"I'll help you there," I said. "That's different."

He let me go in with no more questions. I knew he was on a fool's errand.

I had a headache, and I felt my stomach convulse. Hadn't my father told me not to eat so many peaches?

CHAPTER 21

The Setup

I stepped inside and went straight to bed.

As soon as I was on my mattress, tears poured from my eyes and wet my pillow. I cried because my life was a mess. Eleni's marriage to Panos was a fiasco, but I'd said I would support it. Adrianna had gone away with her husband, and my mother was in the village. Even Andrew's absence bothered me. On top of that, those fellows out there meant it when they said they expected me to help them assassinate a professor.

I stayed awake for hours, thinking about that conspiracy in which I had let myself get involved. Was it true that I was going to help Theodor get rid of Massos? I had never liked that guerilla, and, come to think of it, I really had no quarrel with Massos. True, he had slapped me, but that was months ago. Meanwhile, my grades had improved, and my aptitude for history impressed him. Despite his occasional taunts, I had a vague feeling that he liked me, although why he did, I couldn't imagine. I had done poorly enough in my exams last semester. He had reason enough to flunk me. Why didn't he?

But when I remembered the hungry guests of the wedding party that afternoon, my conscience again pricked me. It was because of Massos and his kind that these people were starving. With the help of the squealers, he organized the searching parties (I had heard this at the meetings) that stole food that could save the lives some of these people. How did the Italians know where to look? They had raided Grandfather's place more than once. These searches had grown into epidemic proportions lately; I heard my father say so at the table, but it was Andrew who had confirmed those suspicions. He always said informers were his best customers; when they helped the Italians to find the wheat, more wheat was in demand. That way, he was getting rich.

But even Andrew had lambasted the squealers, as they were commonly known. They were the most hated people among us; they had turned against their own. And Massos, a Greek professor, was running the operation for the Italians. He had never said such a thing in front of us, of course. He always palavered—though less and less - of late, I had to admit—how the Greeks needed a superior civilization to come to their rescue. That was his main theme, and he had developed a knack for it. Worse yet, some naive students had started believing him. I was told by Stephan that was the root of Fascism.

Now, he was a marked man, and I was in possession of a secret concerning his upcoming assassination. The thought made the few hairs growing on my face stand up. I could feel their hardness. I turned on the mattress, and when I finally fell asleep, I had a dream: I was picking at a skeleton with my fingers, trying to eat any meat that could be found between its ribcage bones. The skeleton sprang to life, caught me by the neck with its bony fingers, and tried to strangle me.

My father told me in the morning that I was screaming all night. "What was the matter with you?" he wanted to know.

"I had a bad dream," I said and left for school without breakfast.

Two days passed, and I managed to see nobody. I arrived at class just as the bell rang and ran away both at noon and at the end of the day, avoiding the urgent looks of some of my fellow students, especially Panos, who tried to get hold of me but couldn't manage. He knocked on the door at night, but I didn't answer.

Fortunately, my mother came back the second morning. It was Tuesday, and I was surprised to see her in the house at noon. I ran to kiss her, to her utter delight. She was happy to see me behave as if I loved her, and she prepared me a nice meal of wheat-and-milk mush that she had brought from the village. It was warm and nutritious, and it gave me more pleasure because of the care with which she prepared it than because I was fed properly.

My mother's being in the house saved me from Panos—I brushed him off once or twice by saying she wouldn't let me out of the house at night. He finally handed me a note—he had scribbled that his wedding had been postponed, this time for good. Eleni's father had suddenly called her back to the village. It was true that Eleni had disappeared from class that morning.

On Wednesday, I couldn't help an encounter with Theodor and Stephan. It was another cold morning; a sharp wind was blowing from the north, and both were bundled up. Principal Albanezi and Torri, accompanied by Massos, were entering the building, and I stood stiffly and delivered the Fascist salute as they passed by. Only Albanezi responded, raising his right hand in a limp gesture.

I heard Theodor's sarcastic voice: "The big boys take their breakfast late." He and Stephan had sneaked up from behind me, and I hadn't had time to run away. "Let's step inside," Theodor said. He wore a white-and-blue-striped woolen cap. Stephan's face was partially covered by a woolen scarf that was wrapped several times around his neck.

I followed them, unable to find an excuse to run away.

"Why the hell are you avoiding us?" Theodor asked, his voice low but threatening.

"My mother is in the house," I said, unable to think of another excuse—that was true anyway.

"This will have to be snappy," he continued, as if he hadn't heard me. "Panos told me you found a sword in hole. Is that true?"

"Yes," I said, surprised they had kept me to ask such a trivial question.

"Where is that sword?"

"In the basement of a house near the bayfront."

"Will you do a little job for us—for our country?"

His face had a pleading look, so I said yes.

"All right, here's what you'll do: during lunch break, get the sword and throw the scabbard into the sea. Then take the blade to your house and hide it there. At seven tonight, meet Panos outside your door with the sword. He will tell you what to do next." He patted me on the shoulder as if to express his complete confidence in me.

I loathed his touching me for a reason I could not fathom. "I'm not sure I can get out at night," I protested, determined now *not* to do what he asked me. "My mother keeps tabs on me."

"Fuck your mother. This job's got to be done."

"What if I can't do it?"

"If you don't go along, I'll see to it that your father hears all about your activities in this group."

"But I haven't had any activities."

"It makes no difference. I'll tell him you have." Theodor drew a tablecloth-size handkerchief with red patches on it out of his pocket and blew his nose. Then he walked away, leaving me there with Stephan.

"What does that guerilla want from me?" I moaned. "I don't understand his instructions."

"Do exactly as he says. Panos will tell you the rest. It's a delicate operation, organized down to a T. Your contribution is minor—but crucial."

"What does he want with an old rusted sword? I heard he has a gun."

"He does. But the idea of the sword appeals to him. It's a sure thing—noiseless, something nobody would ever suspect was used. Despite what he said, Theodor appreciates what you are doing. He thinks highly of you." As if to validate his remarks, he too patted me on the shoulder and then went back inside.

I disliked being patted on the shoulder by him too. What was I? A mama's boy?

My first class that morning was with Manodis, the French teacher. He was still spotlessly dressed in a black suit, starched collar, geometric bowtie, and patent leather shoes. His seeming affluence in a war-torn town was a puzzle. Some evil tongues had it that Manodis was a collaborator too; others said he was in the underground and somebody was slipping him gold pounds. But most of us had no clue because he led a monastic life and never was seen outside of his quarters at Averoff, except to walk to school and back.

Today, Manodis was in rare form, torrentially vocal, pacing about the room as if walking on a tightrope. His clean-shaven face beamed, his voice was fine-tuned, and his garrulous French tongue was loose. It was a joy to hear him lecture, if you wanted to learn French.

But as soon as he started talking, my mind strayed. How had I managed to get myself into such a pass? I was in cahoots with a rebel, and I was helping and abetting him in murdering a teacher. Despite what all those fellows said at the meetings, I had not the slightest proof that Massos was the man who had organized the squealers. Why should a professor stoop to such turpitude? His taunts against the Greeks could have been theoretical. Lots of Greeks criticized each other. Some of my uncles, who descended from the villages to buy supplies, always blasted the Greek banks for not giving them loans. Even if Massos liked the Italians and spoke in their favor, did that make him a traitor who actively sought the starvation of his countrymen?

But even assuming he was as bad as Theodor made him out to be, should I play a role in the plot to assassinate him? As had happened last night, I felt the hairs on my skin stiffen all over my body. My hair must have stood on end because a boy sitting next to me looked at me with his eyes bulging in horror, as if I had turned into a ghost.

No, this was no game. Theodor meant it when he said he was going to get me into serious trouble with my father if I didn't cooperate, and that was the last thing I wanted. I was in a tight spot, and if I was to get out of it, I'd have to come up with a first-rate idea. I racked my brain, thinking hard, paying no attention to Manodis and his lecture. The bell rang, and we all walked downstairs for the noon break.

Stephan's mother was waiting for him at the gate with his scarf, gloves, and overcoat. I said hello to him as she unloaded nuts and raisins into his pockets. He nodded to me that he wanted to talk, but I pretended I didn't see his signal and walked away, stopping for a moment at the kiosk to buy a cone of roasted chickpeas. I munched some, but they were hot from the coals, and I scalded my tongue a bit. I didn't notice Theodor, who had sneaked up behind me, until he dipped his fingers in my cone and picked several of my chickpeas.

"Listen," he said, grinding the chickpeas with his crooked, yellow teeth, "from now on, we mustn't be seen together. Pretend you don't even know me."

"What good would that do? You are already talking to me."

He was annoyed I had argued with him. "I'm being followed right now, and I don't want you to be suspected on my account," he said in a softer tone. "Bring the sword out at seven, as we have agreed."

He peered at me curiously with his blurry, lashless eyes, and, in a funny way, I thought he was trying to be protective of me. "Come on—cheer up, old buddy," he said, again patting me on the shoulder. "We're doing this for our country. Don't you like being useful? Are you going to let that Fascist bastard who slapped you in your face get away with his crimes?"

I said nothing and started walking toward home.

But he caught up with me and grabbed me by the sleeve. "Listen," he said, sounding contrite. "I'm sorry I said that about your mother. I didn't mean to—"

"How about what you said about my father? Will you tell on me?"

"I have no choice."

This time, I shook him for good and ran away. When I reached my doorstep, I changed direction and walked to the old house at the bayfront, where a few weeks ago, Panos and I had found the blade. I knew Panos had bribed Nionios and Avantamos with some scraps of leather and half a loaf of bread to prevent them from stealing the sword. Yiannis Skepitsas hadn't been seen around for days, and nobody knew whether he was drunk in the gutter or dead.

I had only an hour for lunch, so I had to hurry. I turned the corner and came out of the alley and onto the open wharf, feeling the sharp wind in my face. There was no one around. I removed the loose brick from the wall, put my hand inside the hole, and pulled the sword out. Rust lay thick on the sheath, but the blade shone like a mirror. I walked over to the edge of the wharf and tossed the heavy sheath as far as I could into the murky waters of the canal. Nobody saw me.

I trotted home, only a block away, hiding the blade under my overcoat as best as I could. I slipped upstairs unnoticed, but I was taking a big chance. Fortunately, my father wasn't home yet.

My mother, who was in the kitchen, preparing lunch, did hear me and cried out, "Is that you, Philios?"

"Yes, Mother," I replied, out of breath.

"You can come downstairs. Your lunch is ready."

"In a second, Mother."

I had to be quick. I took the blade from under my coat and hid it under the mattress, making sure the bedclothes were left unruffled. My heart was racing. I sat on my desk and printed on a piece of paper: TONIGHT, AN ATTEMPT WILL BE MADE ON YOUR LIFE. BE ALERT. A FRIEND.

"Philios!" my mother's voice rang out again.

"Coming, Mother!"

I folded the note and put it in the pocket of my coat. I ran downstairs and sat in front of the plate of bean soup and fried sardines that my mother had prepared for me. The soup was hot and spicy, just what I needed to warm up. I grabbed a piece of bread, dipped it into the soup, and ate with good appetite.

"What were you doing upstairs?" my mother asked.

"Nothing, Mother. I have a big exam tomorrow, and I had to find some of my notes. I'll have to go out tonight to study with Panos."

"But you've studied so much already," my mother said, looking suspiciously at me.

"Well, I've got lots of exams," I said insolently. I wasn't afraid of her. Fortunately, my father was, as always, busy at his shop at night, so I only had to invent a cheap excuse for my mother.

"Don't forget your scarf and mittens," she said to me in a resigned manner, as I was about to leave the house.

I ran to the school and upstairs into the classroom, just as the one-o'clock class was about to begin. Massos walked in, and I stood up with the rest of the students to give the Fascist salute. Today, his lecture was on Ancient Greek history, and the class listened, absorbed. The subject was Leonidas, a Greek hero who had stood against the vastly superior forces at Thermopylae.

"The Persians never would have crossed," he reflected in a low tone of voice. "Xerxes's elite corps, the Sacred Battalion, had been driven back several times, unable to take the narrow pass. The Greeks fought like lions; they were unconquerable. But then, Ephialtes, a Greek traitor, guided the Persian troops through a narrow gorge, and they attacked from the rear. Three hundred Spartans fell to the last, obedient to the laws of their motherland."

This was a strange speech, coming from Massos at this moment, but my mind took a different path. I would have to slip the note into his hands. Massos's overcoat, with his leather gloves stuck in one of its pockets, rested on a chair behind the podium.

It occurred to me that the coat would remain there during the ten-minute recess, while Massos and the students emptied the classroom for that time. Massos then would return from his office to continue lecturing on another subject.

When the bell rang, I remained in my seat, pretending to tie my shoelaces and waiting for everyone to clear the room. All left except Stephan, who saw my delay and lingered to ask me a question.

"Listen," he said, "did you understand that you and Panos are supposed to pick me up tonight?"

"I didn't understand anything of the sort," I said rudely. "Theodor only told me to go with Panos and follow his instructions. He didn't say anything about picking you up."

"Well, the plan has changed. After you meet Panos, you come

to my house. I have some problems at home, of which you know nothing."

I suddenly hated the guy. I was sure he couldn't leave his house without his mother's permission. What kind of a man was he, posing as a hero who couldn't even cheat his mother?

But I was careful not to show any of these feelings. I was anxious about my own plan.

"All right, we'll be there to pick you up," I said, wishing he would leave the room.

But he hung on, looking at me. "Did you do as Theodor said?" he asked.

"Yes," I said, still tying my shoelaces.

Stephen seemed curious about my activity. He kept looking at me, as I was still not moving, but finally, he left the room.

Without delay, I jumped from my seat and quickly inserted the note into one of the pockets of the overcoat, the one free of gloves.

I rushed out of the room and almost bumped against Massos, who was just reentering it. He didn't say anything, though he gave me a puzzled look. My hands felt freezing as I walked downstairs. No matter what happened, I was sure I would be caught.

CHAPTER 22

The Traitor

It was about seven o'clock when Panos picked me up. My mother had refused to let me go out by myself. She had told my father that afternoon of my repeated absences, and he had issued orders that I couldn't go out unless escorted by someone she trusted. When Panos showed up at the door, pleading that we wouldn't go farther than next door, my mother gave in, but she didn't look quite convinced I'd go study.

"Come back in an hour," she said.

I nodded, and a few moments later, Panos and I walked out into the cold March night. The clouds had hung low all day, and the chill in the air froze my finger. Some leaf-sized white flakes were already twisting and flapping through the air before touching the frozen ground.

I was bundled up, wearing a woolen cap and a scarf wrapped around my neck several times. I'd stuffed the mittens my mother had insisted I take along into one of my pockets, leaving my hands free to squeeze the blade against my chest. It dangled uncomfortably and caused me to walk stiffly, slowing down Panos's rapid step. I had slipped by my mother's watchful eye, pretending I carried books under my elbow. I don't know to what extent my mother, whom I had tricked so many times, had been fooled. Certainly, she couldn't have imagined I was carrying a sword!

Panos, also well bundled up but hatless, walked beside me. As we came to the end of the alley before the tiny square of St. Paraskevi, Panos stopped.

"Listen," he said, "I must tell you something. Tomorrow night is the night. Eleni and I are eloping. Everything has been arranged."

"But Eleni is back at the village."

"We managed to communicate. A friend of mine who owns a taxicab—I had to pay him a roll of leather—will drive me to her village. She'll wait at the end of the road. I'll pick her up. A monk at the monastery will be waiting for us."

I always thought him mad and now madder than ever. But I was willing to forgive him his madness if he'd leave me out of his schemes.

"So what do you want of me?" I said, my heart as cold as the snow that was falling.

"What do I want from you? Nothing," he said with contempt.

"I'll go along if you tell me."

He had started walking again but now stopped short, and even in the darkness, I could sense he was looking at me with curiosity. After all, I always thought him to be chicken-hearted, not even capable of holding a grudge.

"We'll all come back to town," he said. "The ceremony will take place at Agios Menas Church, secretly. It won't last longer than half an hour."

"How did you manage?"

"It took a lot of … leather. The monks wear shoes too."

"I'll be there. You can count on me."

He shook my hand, and we started walking again. I didn't really feel sorry for Panos, nor did I have any real desire to help him. I just wanted everything to be over and done with.

We walked a few more blocks, and just before we reached the town square, next to Mataphias's tavern, Panos drew me aside into a narrow lane.

"This is where we part," he said.

"Why?" I said, not liking the idea of walking by myself in the dark night.

"The carabinieri are all over the place, and two people are more visible than one. Besides, I have my instructions for what each of us must do. Here's your part: you go to Stephan's house and knock on his door. That's the signal for him to come out. His mother will give him permission to go out only if she sees you there. You will go with him. Meanwhile, I will go to the corner on Saint Menas's street, where Theodor will be waiting with two other fellows for the rest of us to show up. At eight o'clock sharp, Massos leaves his house to go to Manodis's, where the two of them play cards. They're buddies, I was told. On the way there, he will be ambushed and killed outside the church, just as he turns the corner."

I heard all this as I was shaking with cold and terror. Panos had told me those words in a whisper, and I was amazed by what he had said. Massos would be assassinated outside the same church where Panos planned to get married the next night. In my eyes, Panos had turned out to be both a maniac and a hero. What was I becoming by helping him? God Almighty!

"Now, give me the sword," Panos said.

I disentangled the thing from inside my coat and gave it to him. "What if Stephan's mother doesn't let him go out?" I murmured, unable to find anything else to say.

"Just knock on the door. He will come out."

Stephan's house was at the other end of town, so I had to walk quite a distance. I almost turned around several times, but my momentum kept me going forward. I reached the town square, where a few young couples were still strolling up and down, despite the cold weather and the upcoming curfew. The men were too busy looking at the girls to pay much attention to me, and the few carabinieri who stood at the corners were also preoccupied with the passing female forms.

I darted across the square and into a dark alley, hoping nobody had noticed me. The snow fell thick and melted immediately, turning into mud in the puddles, most which were invisible in the darkness. I was wearing galoshes over my shoes, but my feet were already damp and freezing.

As I crossed into the next alley, I smelled the sweet aroma of doughnuts and cinnamon coming from the shop of Gerasimos, who served his customers the best rice pudding in town. Gerasimos, a distant relative, had failed in business in Athens and had come to the island during the war. Now, he was dealing on the black market. His doughnut shop was a front for selling liquor and making profits.

I bumped against a man who had just come out of the door of the shop, looking half drunk. He was my uncle Costas, one of my father's cousins, who worked for him at the shop. He was known for his drinking habits.

"Where are you going at this hour, my champ?" he said, recognizing me. In the faint light that came from Gerasimos's window, I saw him smiling maliciously at me. Costas was a close friend of my father's, but I detested him. He had always made crude jokes about my poor grades and wisecracked that my lack of height damaged my chances with girls.

"I'm going to study at a friend's," I responded, determined not to let him stop me.

"Not so fast, my champ," he said and stood in front of me. "Your father might like to know where his sonny is wandering, so far from home at this time of night."

I tried to side-step him, but he grabbed me by the ear, which his finger found inside the folds of my scarf. He twisted my ear savagely and pulled me the opposite way. I almost screamed with the pain. I knew he intended to take me back home like that and then brag to my father that he had caught me. He kept smiling at me wickedly, sure of his strength.

I gave him a sudden push, and, as he was barely sober, he staggered back. I freed myself from his grasp, though my ear almost came off in his hand, and started running. I ran for two blocks, and then I stopped to catch my breath. Obviously, he was too drunk to catch up with me.

I was late, so I started running again and didn't stop until I was in front of Stephan's house. I saw lights; the door was open, and carabinieri were going in and out. Before I knew what was happening, Panos came out of a dark alley and grabbed me by the arm.

"Let's go back," he whispered, pulling me away. "Theodor has been arrested."

"What?" I said, astonished, as he pulled me into the alley.

"The carabinieri took him from his house half an hour ago. They just went into Stephan's house and picked him up too. I thought you had gone in. What kept you?"

I didn't tell him, being too scared even to talk, but I followed him as he tiptoed cautiously, peering around corners to see if the street was clear.

"What did you do with the sword?" I asked as soon as I got a chance.

"It's been disposed of. Let's hurry back."

"What do you think happened?"

"Someone squealed."

"Who knew about this?"

"Some people did," Panos said, obviously in no mood for explanations. He started running again.

I tried to keep pace with him, but my galoshes splashed into the puddles, and I soon began to drag my feet. Nobody seemed to be following us, so I slowed down, letting him run ahead of me. I was dead tired, and besides, who knew what kind of reception waited for me at home after my encounter with that abominable Costas. I was probably in for a bashing.

I reached home, breathless and looking muddy. My mother saw me out of breath, but I mumbled some excuse or other, and she let me go to bed, happy I was back safe.

The next morning was again very cold, but the sky was cloudless. I went directly to my Latin class, for which I had not prepared. The teacher, Mrs. Kontopreah, who had replaced Massos for this course, was a gray-haired elderly woman, who exhibited practically no authority in the classroom. The students talked to each other freely, as if they were in the school cafeteria, and paid no attention to what she said. During her lecture, the boys and girls spent their time snapping dried pumpkin seeds between their teeth or eating boiled artichokes and carelessly throwing the refuse on the floor. As she walked in front of the podium, she stepped on the spiked leaves and dry shells that had already formed a carpet, and it made a sound as if she'd walked on broken crockery. With every step, she provoked another giggle from the class, and the chaos kept growing. The poor woman didn't say anything; she was too intimidated by her male students, especially Theodor, who usually sat in the first row, ostentatiously sharpening his pencils with his butcher knife.

But Theodor was absent this morning, and so was Stephan. Panos, Chalimourdas, and another fellow who had been at the meeting were in their seats, though. I had no chance to talk to any of them, having arrived late. The cold, which had intensified during the night, penetrated the thick stone walls, freezing our hands and feet. Pale and shivering, Mrs. Kontopreah had begun to scrawl Latin words on the blackboard when the classroom door banged open, and Principal Albanezi, with two armed carabinieri, rumbled in.

"Rise!" he howled, before we had time to recover from our astonishment. "All up!" he barked again.

We all rose and gave the Fascist salute.

He paced back and forth in the room one or twice, like a wild animal in a cage. He was a small man, but he had a barrel chest, which he kept inflating by taking deep breaths, and he moved his arms to the sides as he walked, in the manner of a breast-stroke swimmer. He stopped abruptly, made a turn, and faced us.

"This is abominable!" he barked. "This is something you'll pay for, you shameless Greeklings!"

He raved and choked, and his face turned to dark purple—I thought he was having a stroke. But then he grew suddenly calm. His features assumed an expression of sublime compassion, and he explained, "An attempt was made against the life of Professor Massos last night. Fortunately, it was thwarted in time. The guilty have been captured and will be punished. But there are others who remain at large, conspirators against the well-being of the noble Italian Empire. They, too, will be arrested momentarily."

Once more, he paced back and forth, stopped, and looked at us with a curious smile on his face. "But before I arrest the others, you must know this: a warning was issued to your teacher yesterday, thus saving his life. We do not know who the person is, but we have reason to believe he is in this room. We would like to commend him. Let him come forward."

A stunned silence prevailed; all breaths were instantly suspended. I kept my eyes lowered and my fists clenched. Now what? Could anyone suspect me? I caught sight of Panos, who sat directly across from me; he was staring hard at me. My heart was beating fast, and perspiration covered my face, despite the cold.

"*Basta*!" Albanezi shouted and motioned to the carabinieri.

The two of them rushed to the back of the room and seized Chalimourdas, who was strong, as rugged as an oak tree, and had vise-like hands that could crack your skull like a nut. When a much shorter Italian attempted to lay his hands on him, Chalimourdas pushed him back so hard he threw the man topsy-turvy over one of the benches. But the other soldier struck him with the butt of his rifle, breaking his nose and jaw. Blood spurted from the fellow's mouth, and the girls screamed.

Albanezi barked, and more carabinieri rushed in and grabbed Chalimourdas, who was still resisting, pushing them away like so many cardboard boxes. Finally, they subdued him. They took him out with another student—the husky fellow I had seen at the meeting—and Panos, who gave me an agonized look as he was being dragged away. It took me a full five minutes to realize that nothing was going to happen to me and that I was safe.

CHAPTER 23

Remorse

A month and a half went by. It was now early May, a morning of unbroken blue sky and bright sunshine. I decided to skip class and go to Vardania with Avantamos. Older than most of us, Avantamos had failed for years to pass to the next grade, growing middle-aged in high school. In class, Avantamos was the picture of apathy. He never studied, never asked a question, and never answered when asked. For his apathy, he was nicknamed the "existentialist," though he hardly knew what that name meant. He was so serious in his pursuit of laziness that he almost was respected for it.

He and I took off for Vardania, where I would watch him spend his morning setting traps for goldfinches or spearing water snakes and frogs. He'd sell the goldfinches to pet bird collectors in town to earn some income, enough to keep his mother and sister from starving.

For my part, I had my reasons for playing hooky that day. I had heard that Theodor had been transferred from the jail in town to the prison, which was located near Vardania, and I hoped I could catch a glimpse of him. The fact that he was brought to Vardania prison meant that he probably would be taken to Preveza for trial in the martial court. What would happen to him after that was anybody's guess. My father, who had heard his story, speculated it was either the firing squad or the dungeons at Janina, from which few people ever came out alive. Panos, Stephan, Chalimourdas, and the husky young man were all released within a week of their arrests and had returned to school. There was no evidence against them, and, besides, their parents had money, and the Italians could be bribed. Theodor had no relatives, and no one knew where he had come from. He lived with Olga, my godmother, who rented rooms near the marketplace and whom Theodor called his "aunt." When asked, Olga stated to the carabinieri that she knew nothing about him except that he had paid his rent regularly.

As for me, nobody had bothered me or seemed to suspect my involvement in the gang. Costas had not reported his encounter with me to my father, probably embarrassed by his clumsy attempt to capture me. My midterm exams had ended with good results; I passed both Ancient Greek and history, the subjects Massos taught, with high grades, to the total surprise of my father.

Massos himself had changed; he now refrained from his anti-Greek tirades in class and behaved in a subdued and distant manner, intent on just doing his job. We heard that at the end of this semester, he was being transferred to another school in a different province. So, all was well. Only Panos had hinted, a few days after his release, that he knew who had warned Massos. I didn't press him for details, and he did not elaborate. His elopement with Eleni had been a fiasco. After he got out of jail, he had made me wait for him and her at the corner at St. Menas Church—the spot of the aborted attempt against Massos's life.

I waited for an hour, but nobody showed up. He told me later that her father had heard of his plan and had shut Eleni in his house for good. She was never to come back to town. All her plans to finish her education were ruined, thanks to him. Panos never heard another word from her, though he tried. I guessed what a blow this was for him, and he never brought up the subject of Eleni again.

Avantamos and I reached the prison building, an old gray fort covered with moss and lichen and surrounded by a foul-smelling ditch. The pavement ended at this point, and the dirt road was filled with all sorts of junk—broken iron bands, pieces of rusty brown wire, and flattened-out tin cans buried in the dust. I stopped for a moment near the prison wall and kicked an empty can, sending dust up in a cloud.

Avantamos, who had gone ahead of me by about thirty yards, ran back toward me, moving his hands in the air. He looked ecstatic.

"Did you hear?" he cried, excited. "The new goldfinches have arrived!" Where goldfinches were concerned, Avantamos was an aesthete, capable of listening to their warbling for hours on end.

At that moment, we heard a whistle, signaling that a group of prisoners were being brought out of their cells for their morning walk on the flat roof of the prison. They were burly-looking fellows and wore prisoners' caps and striped uniforms. They strolled about leisurely, smoking cigarettes, evidently enjoying this bright, beautiful day.

Then, one of them broke away from his group and leaned against the edge of the wall, directly above where I stood. I recognized Theodor instantly. His curly red hair showed from under his cap, and his beard had grown grotesquely, covering his face like a dark-purple, bushy plant. As he leaned over the wall, smoking his cigarette, he caught sight of me. He knew who I was right away, and the discovery brightened his face.

"How is it going, old buddy?" he said in his gravelly voice, the sound of which I remembered.

"All right," I said, not certain how to respond.

"I hear you're finally getting rid of the bastard," he said again.

"He is going to another town," I responded, catching his meaning.

"That's good," he said. "You did a fine job." He snapped his middle finger outwards against his thumb, and the cigarette butt made an arc and fell in front of me, extinguishing itself in the brine with a hiss. "Take care," he said. Then he walked away.

A squadron of scissor-tailed goldfinches flew overhead, filling the cloudless blue sky with their crystalline twittering.

I saw Avantamos standing on a bank that rose above the muddy path streaking through the bulrushes, some fifty yards away. He was getting ready to set one of his traps. He looked ecstatic.

"Come over!" he thundered, waving his hand.

But I didn't move. A pang of guilt stabbed me like a knife, right then and there. Had I not sent that man to prison, possibly to his death? Would I see him again, ever, to ask forgiveness? I sat down on the dust, brought my knees up to my face, and sobbed.

PART III

The Return

CHAPTER 24

A Meeting

I stepped off the bus, two suitcases by my side, and tried to flag down a taxicab. It was hot, and the asphalt burned under my feet. I was exhausted after my five-hour bus trip from Athens. Five, ten minutes passed before, finally, a cab stopped and picked me up.

I gave the driver the address of an apartment I had rented for me and my family, who were coming later in July; we needed a place to stay. I had written to my father from the States, asking him to make this arrangement, and he was more than happy to oblige. I also called him from Athens and asked him not to announce my arrival to our relatives for the first few days. He argued a bit, eager as he was to make my arrival an event, but he promised he would do as I said for the time being.

I rested a few hours, and, later in the afternoon I went to visit him and explained to him that I wanted to spend a few days alone in one of the beach villages on the west end of the island, as I was writing a book of my memories of the war, and I needed some time to reflect and map out the book design.

The old man, who had come to the States to visit us the year before, understood my reasons for not announcing my arrival right away. He himself had helped me by allowing me to tape his memories of the war, so I had materials that I could use from his side of the story, and he had given me his permission to use these notes as I saw fit. My mother had died soon after the war, and my father's second wife, Sophia, a nice middle-aged lady I had already met, brought us coffee and rolls at the table outside in his yard, under his trellised vine, and he and I chatted for a while.

I left him mumbling to himself and returned to the apartment and had a plain meal of salami and cheese sandwich and plenty of fruit that my cousin, Aristos, the owner of the apartment, had filled the refrigerator with. Jet-lagged as I was, I slept the entire night and part of the morning, but I got up well rested and raring to go. The same cab driver came to pick me up and drove me to Ai-Yiannis, a beach a few kilometers west of town, where owners of the fields in the nearby villages were renting cabins, mostly to tourists.

The driver had spotted me for an American right away, though I spoke Greek to him, and asked me how things were in the States.

"Just fine," I responded laconically.

He reminded me that a travel advisory had been issued to American tourists, which had damaged the Greek economy. "Greece lost three hundred thousand jobs this year."

I doubted his statistic but refrained from making a comment, not wanting to be drawn into a political argument. He kept jabbering, seemingly disgruntled by his inability to elicit a lengthier response from me. But he went away with a broad grin when I paid him in dollars—I explained that I hadn't had a chance to go to the bank yet.

"They'll skewer you if you go to them," he attested. "I have a relative who can give you a better exchange rate." He drove off, whistling "Rock-a-Bye Baby." He had been in Brooklyn.

Ai-Yiannis was located at the northern end of a mountain range that ran the length of the island, descending in graded slopes and knots, until it crept into the sea. The beach was a narrow strip of sand, guarded on the western side by windy bluffs and dotted with boulders, which probably had rolled down from the heights after an earthquake. A peculiarity of this beach was that one could dig a hole with one's hand in the sand and see the water spurt out, forming a pool from which a small stream ran toward the sea. The water in these holes was a little briny but drinkable. In older times, fishermen dug pools the size of a twelve-foot crater, into which they released the mullet they caught with their nets. The fish swam in the brine, thus staying fresh until a buyer came along. I remembered watching those mullet when I was a boy and had come to the place with my father, who did business with the fishermen, building their cabins.

No pools were there now. The fishermen had been hired by the big fishing boats in the harbor or gone into some other business. The place had changed. If anything, it had become more desolate than when I knew it before. But it had a reputation for its wild beauty, and, though still unknown to most tourists, several locals had built a few cabins that they rented to those who wanted to spend their vacations there with their families.

When I arrived in late morning, a man in charge of the cottages led me to my cabin, which my cousin had reserved for me, and I paid him the rent—fifty dollars for an entire week.

By noon, I was settled in my cabin. The man who owned it had been charged with bringing me food three times a day. My first meal consisted of fried red mullet, tomato salad, feta cheese, and bread—just enough for my simplified tastes. He also brought me a bottle of white wine. A couple of glasses of that, plus a lingering jet lag, made me too groggy to resist a nap. Besides, the heat was rising. I fell on the hard mattress, which had been laid on boards mounted on two wooden tripods and slept for several hours.

When I awoke, the sun had dipped behind the western cliffs, leaving elongated shadows on the sands. The sea was a sheet of dazzling azure-emerald, striped with foamy crests that spent themselves on the beach.

I took a stroll to the base of a rock, where the waves had formed a natural cave that was strewn with seaweed and pebbles, which had been rounded and polished by the action of the waves—"dove's eggs," the locals called them.

On my way back, I dipped into the waves, already having second thoughts about my vacation. I tried to think of the sequence of the chapters for my novel, but nothing came to my mind—except a patch of confused and perplexing ideas. Why had I come here, leaving my father alone during my first visit to the place of my birth? The death of my mother had shaken him up, but he had found, of late, some peace of mind. Sophia was taking good care of him, and he looked happy and content. But my abrupt departure had bothered him, and I felt I had been insensitive to his feelings.

There was another reason for my uneasiness. Despite its rugged beauty, the beach suddenly looked desolate. What would I do here, all by myself for an entire week? I felt a little silly with the grand idea I had formed in my head about blissful solitude (in imitation of Thoreau, the subject of my doctoral dissertation) next to the waves. After all, what was the use of being a grown man—no doubt of my middle years—and a professor if I could not rid myself of such foggy impulses?

My night passed in physical discomfort. I thought the mattress was infested with vermin because I felt the need to scratch several times. I had always been scared of rats and cockroaches and squirmed when I thought of them.

But in the morning, when I saw the sun break over Mount Lamia in the east, I felt refreshed. I jogged along the beach and took another dip in the cool—but not cold—water. I dug a hole near my cabin and watched the water fill it, and I washed my face in it. I drank some of it, using a tin cup the fisherman had given me; it had a strong briny taste—probably good for my digestion.

The second morning was more enjoyable than the first. All the troubles of life, its little annoyances, had flown away—for the moment, at least. I strolled along the sand close to the boulders, swam, and then had a simple lunch at noon, followed by a delicious nap. The chapter sequences arrived clearly, and that gave me the direction I needed. I had already written the middle part of the novel and called it *"The Traitor"*, and I could use the first part, "Bonds of War," to tell of my very early years, when I went to school and the war came, destroying lives and altering normality, and people agonized through it. For nearly five years of my early life, I'd lived in a conquered country—a slave, if you ask me. Those early years I never forgot; they always haunted me. Now, I had a chance to recount them.

I wondered about the ending of my story. Symmetry, the logic of a finale that a reader would expect, escaped me. But then again, had my story ended? If there was to be a sequel, what would that be? Puzzling questions—but for the time being, I let them be. I had a delicious lunch and took a nap.

When I awoke and looked outside the cabin, the sun was still high, its rays falling almost vertically, burning the sands. The few trees on the cliff above the rocks had wilted, though the buzz of the cicadas nesting in them had intensified. I leaned against the wall of my cabin and gazed at the waveless water in the distance, unable to think or feel.

Gradually, my eyes rested on a man sitting at the base of the rock, in the shade, about a hundred yards away. I looked again. What could he be doing out there in that inferno?

I managed to muster enough energy to walk out of the cabin. The sand scorched my feet, the sun blistered my skin, my eyes were blinded in the glare, and a sheet of lava twisted and burned in the air. I was overwhelmed.

I staggered to the spot where the man sat. He was a fellow in his middle years, heavily built, squared-faced with a squashed nose, and short, straight red hair that was turning gray. He wore a long-sleeved tartan shirt that was, despite the heat, buttoned to his neck. He was holding a bundle of typewritten sheets in his hands, seeming intent on memorizing their contents.

The cave, at that point, ended in a wall of half-buried boulders that blocked passage to the other side. I turned around, but by that time, I was standing next to the man.

I decided to greet him. "Hello."

"Hello!" he said, springing to his feet and offering to shake my hand. A limp handshake between us followed. "How are you?" he asked, as if we were acquaintances.

"I'm fine," I responded.

"Don't you remember me?"

"I'm afraid I don't."

"We were classmates!" he exclaimed, sounding impatient with my memory lapse. "We were in the same class, during the war. It has been"—he counted on his fingers—"twenty-six years!"

"What is your name?" I asked.

"Theodor."

"Theodor?"

"Yes, yes. I went to prison, remember?"

"*That* Theodor?"

"Yes, yes. Remember now?"

"You have changed. You have changed enormously. I just couldn't have recognized you at all."

"Well, it's been a long time. And I've gone through a lot."

"I still can't believe it's you. You had curly hair. Now your hair is straight. Your nose wasn't that flat then."

"I went into prizefighting. As for my hair, at that time I was underground, and I had my hair curled with a hot iron to escape identification. Appearances, you know, are deceiving. But I'm the same person, nonetheless."

"Are you?" I said, shaking his hand for the second time. I was struck by his sudden appearance and wasn't certain whether it would be wise to go on talking to him. But I didn't want to show lack of courtesy, so I asked him, "How has life treated you?"

"Well … not bad, overall. I've had my ups and downs—or downs and ups, I should say."

"How did you get—free?"

He gave me a meaningful smile, revealing a set of yellow and crooked teeth. "That was something. The Italians arrested me, tried me, convicted me as a rebel, and were about to execute me. But as they were transferring me to Janina for that purpose, I jumped from the van in which they were carrying me and some of my fellow inmates, when one of our guards fell asleep. Two fellows who escaped with me stepped on a mine as we were going through a minefield and died a couple of hours later. I managed to elude the Italians and Germans who were after me, and later, I joined the forces of General Napoleon Zervas in Epirus.[5] I fought for two years with their detachment and was decorated twice for bravery."

He said all that with the air of a man who never exaggerated. His potato-like face didn't grow more familiar in my memory as he went on talking. In fact, with the exception of his teeth and his red hair, nothing about him recalled a resemblance. Indeed, I wondered whether I was talking to an ex-classmate or to an impostor.

"Where are you staying?" I asked, looking for a chance to break away.

"Over there," he said, pointing to one of the cabins, two rows down from mine.

"I live in that one." I pointed to it. "Come and join me for dinner later."

"That's extremely nice of you." His smile broadened, and he shook my hand again.

As I walked back to my cabin, a din in my ears warned me I might be having sunstroke. But as soon as I was in the cool cabin, I felt better. I told the caretaker to bring me another stool, as I was expecting a guest. I still couldn't believe that this was Theodor, though twenty-six years can change a man's face.

But there was something else about this fellow that seemed deceptive and out of sync. The point is that he didn't look real. His sudden appearance under the rock had startled me. And he sat there

---

[5] General of the Resistance fighting forces during the four-year occupation of Greece and said to be on the conservative side.

as if he knew I was coming and was waiting for me. He greeted me as if we had said goodbye to each other only yesterday.

I stopped giving the matter much thought. I'd soon have the occasion to find out more about him.

When the caretaker came to take my order for dinner—fried fish, tomato salad, bread, cheese, and a bottle of wine—I ordered one more plate. Just then, the man stepped in.

"Hello," he said with ostentatious warmth and sat down on one of the stools, across from me. I offered him wine in a plastic cup. He took it, toasted to my health, and drank it in one gulp. I noticed how his muscles bulged under his shirt and remembered the husky old Theodor. This fellow looked forty-five or fifty but was still of an athletic build. He resembled a bull that could smash the straw cabin with a charge. But he didn't seem to be in a rage at all; in fact, his face seemed vacant.

"You still don't believe I'm Theodor," he said after a while, when he had drained a second cup.

"Well, I don't want to disbelieve you. It's been so long, and I've been away for many years. It's hard to remember faces."

"Especially this one," he said with a low giggle.

"I mean any face."

"Is this your first trip back from the States?" he asked.

"How did you know I was in the States?"

"Why, it's obvious. You look American—pants, shirt, haircut. You flash that information a mile off. Besides, you are not all that obscure. People have followed your career. Your name was featured in the local press more than once or twice."

He sat there, eating my fried fish, drinking my wine, wishing me health, and talking about my life. I had the impression that my mind was failing to register whatever I heard. Surely, this was a bad dream I was living through. How could it be reality?

"How do you like it back home?" he inquired between bites.

"I don't like tourists."

"I don't see any here."

"That's why I escaped town. I used to come to this place with my classmates on picnics, back when I was a high school student."

"I remember," he said. "I was with you several times."

I looked at him in disbelief. This was going too far. The real Theodor, back then, never mixed with my social group, and I had never seen him outside those brief moments at the gang gatherings and a few times in the street. I had never had anything else to do with him, and he had not lived in our town long enough during the war for me to socialize with him.

"You know, I have been in the States too," he said.

I braced myself for another fib.

"I know you don't believe me, but every word I say is true. I first went to Berkeley, where I got mixed up with some radicals and got jailed after a demonstration during the Cuban missile crisis. I trained to be a boxer, but my career was wrecked when my nose was broken. Then I came to the Midwest, where you happened to be at the time. I remember your teaching at the Circle campus, University of Illinois at Chicago. You gave a lecture on Valaoritis in the Greek Cultural Center at LaSalle and Dearborn. I was there at that lecture."

I was so shocked to hear him say these things that my vision blurred, and beads of perspiration trickled down my spine. How could he have known a detail like that? I had never written to anyone in Greece about that lecture, not even to my father. Unless this fellow actually had been at the event, he couldn't have known about it.

I had no alternative but to listen.

"I stayed in Chicago for a while," he continued, having by this time finished eating all the fish and all the bread and tomatoes. But there was still some wine left, and he was sipping it from the bottle. "I was trying to get admitted at the Circle—and I did and became a member of the Hellenic Club, of which you were the faculty adviser. You held a seminar, at which I was present. You read 'Ithaca' by Cavafy in Greek, and then there was a controversial discussion about Cavafy's homosexuality. In defending the poet, you did rather well, I will admit. You know, I'm a poet myself."

I was in a mental state beyond belief or disbelief. This was not just a live dream but a full-blown nightmare. Nothing could explain the weird sensation I felt in hearing this man and being unable to free myself from the stranglehold he had on me.

"And what do you do now?" I managed to ask.

"I am on the lecture circuit," he replied nonchalantly.

"What lecture circuit?"

"Actually, it's only me," he admitted modestly. "I lecture throughout Greece, in the big cities mainly but sometimes in smaller towns, like this one, for pennies, just because of a certain obligation I have here. I am incorporated by myself."

"That's a contradiction."

"No matter; the title of my lecture is 'Ingratitude Is Radioactivity.' I came to this beach, where it's quiet, to prepare."

I asked no more questions, deciding to go along with the flow of things. I was tired and half drunk.

"I studied physics at Ann Arbor," he went on, adding a fresh twist to his story. "I went there after I left Chicago. I did didn't manage to get my Ph.D. having failed to transfer all my credits from the Circle. You know how things can get at you. I had to settle for lesser goals."

With this, he stopped talking. The bottle was empty in his hand (it was a half-gallon bottle), and he was visibly affected.

The heat outside, meanwhile, had eased, and it was getting late. I leaned over the mattress, found the straw pillow, and dozed off. When I awoke, it was completely dark, and the stranger was gone. I went back to sleep.

CHAPTER 25

The Count

The next morning, the sun's rays coming through the chinks in the cabin woke me. It was a dazzling morning, blue sky and cool enough. The sand beach was inviting, so I ran outside to take a swim before breakfast. When I returned to the cabin, the fisherman was there with a tray of sesame rolls, jam, and coffee and a folded-in half envelope that he took from his pocket.

I grabbed the envelope and opened it. There was a card, on which thick black letters were written: HIS HUMBLENESS THE COUNT THEODOR DE VILAMONTIS INVITES HIS ESTEEMED COLLEAGUE FOR BREAKFAST IN HIS CABIN.

The Count? His Humbleness? What else was there in store for me?

"Show me this man's cabin," I asked the fisherman. He pointed three doors to my left to a cabin that looked abandoned.

I stepped in there, with the fisherman following me with the tray. I found the man I met yesterday sitting on a stool next to his mattress, eating something out of wooden bowl.

"Come in, come in, Professor," he exclaimed when he saw me at his door. He got up and prepared to offer me a seat—nowhere. Indeed, there was no place in his cabin where I could have sat down. Finally, he fussed for nothing, and then offered me his stool. He himself sprawled on the mattress, which had the odor of decaying weed.

"Argyri!" he called out for the fisherman, who still stood at the door with the tray. "Bring us some cheese! And don't forget the eggs!"

The man left my tray on the floor and went away to fill the order. The count, meanwhile, started eating my breakfast, pretending it was his.

"Help yourself," he urged me, sounding generous.

Everything on my tray disappeared before I had time to take a bite.

"Oh," he noticed, "you're not eating. Yesterday's heat must have inhibited your appetite."

"It was hot," I conceded, "but my appetite was not affected."

"You know," he went on, paying no attention to my remarks, "we scholars must have our regular meals. The brain works in quantum leaps during its periodic orgasmic cycles. You know what I mean."

"Indeed, I do," I said, not knowing. I was so offended by his gluttony, his squalor, and his pretentiousness that my mind was reeling. He must have sensed the distaste he had generated in me—I could see that in his eyes.

Argyri came back with a plate, on which there was a slice of white cheese, and a basket with some bread and hard-boiled eggs. I took an egg and started peeling it. I did not want to starve.

"You see," he said, alluding to yesterday's conversation, "not only am I world-traveled, but I also come from an ancient family. Though my father was a shepherd from Acarnania, my mother was noble."

"Oh?" I decided not to believe anything else he said from that point on, having made up my mind that this man was not only a fraud but a lunatic.

"That's where I inherited my title. My grandmother was from Zakynthos, an island where titled landlords still exist—even today—since the time of the Venetians, who granted those titles when they occupied the islands for more than two hundred years."

"But even so, one doesn't inherit a title from one's mother," I protested.

"Oh, no! You don't know the jurisprudence involved here," he exclaimed. "Titles can be inherited any way one prefers; they are bequeathed in a last will and testament to a descendant one pleases to name. My grandmother's husband, Count Alexandros Vilamontis, whose name I retain, gave the title to me, after the death of my mother. I am a count, just as Lord Byron became a lord, from a maternal line. I have legal proof of that. The title was authenticated a long time ago, before I departed for the States. There, I dropped it. In a foreign country, a title sounds odd, you know," he assured me. He was busy with my cheese and ate peeled eggs with the speed of a conveyor belt.

He resumed addressing me, as if I were part of an audience of his. "Anyway, titles don't really interest me for their own sake. It's the loftiness of the intellect that counts!" he burst out triumphantly, proud of his silly pun. "I'm a perpetual student, a dynamic and active scholar, and crowds love me. I tear them apart with my oratory. You will witness this when you come to hear my lecture, a few nights from now."

I had no intention of going to his "lecture," of course, or of hearing more from him or about him.

"You will excuse me," I said, getting up, "but my father expects me in town. I have to go."

"I will send you two tickets," he said, gripping my hand effusively and taking me to the door (which was only a step away). "You will come?"

"Yes, yes," I said hastily, wanting to get away from him. I already felt like he was an escapee from a leper colony.

But he rushed after me with a maniacal leap.

"What's the matter?" he said, and his eyelids raced. "Don't you remember me, Philios? Don't you recall the meeting behind the Skepitsas house? The sword you took out of the basement hole and hid in your house for the assassination? Your coming to Stephan's with Panos and hearing I had been arrested? My staying in that prison for two months? Don't you remember our agreement to get rid of the bastard Massos, who slapped you in the face? Do you know where he is now? He has a job at the University of Salonika! He is a professor of classics there, teaching Greek youth! That's what happens to a bankrupt society. The traitors and criminals live on and prosper and get degrees. You and I, the patriots who sacrificed—who pays attention to us now?"

I managed to get away from his grasp. Sweat was pouring from my face, though it was only midmorning. This was a madman, no doubt, a phony, a con artist. Theodor! Lectures! The garbage man in our town would have had more dignity. I don't know how he got hold of such details of my life as he had, but this was not anyone I had ever known! I was absolutely sure of that.

"Excuse me," I said rather rudely. "I need to go. My father is waiting. I promise to come to your lecture."

"But don't you remember me?" he pleaded, and his grotesque, potato-shaped face reddened with a painful expression. "We were schoolmates. Am I not your friend?"

"I do remember you now," I lied. "But I have to go."

I sent for the taxicab right away, but I had to wait an hour before it arrived to pick me up from town. The same driver was blasting the United States government, saying it sided with Turkey on the question of Cyprus. A few minutes later, he started blasting the Greek government too. They weren't tough enough with the Americans, he claimed. Greece is a US colony and so forth and so on.

Before I left, I paid Argyri for his services, adding twenty dollars to the fifty dollars of our agreement. I couldn't stay for the week, I told him. I had to go. He gazed at me with a microscopic smile, and I added twenty dollars more to his tip. That should have done it.

The count stood at the door of his cabin, watching me as I rode away, and he waved at me with a smile, which revealed his sickening teeth.

I felt a strange pang inside me. What if this fellow was actually Theodor, the man I had betrayed to the Italians so many years ago? Would I have to live through that nightmare again?

CHAPTER 26

The Loan

As I rode back to town, I couldn't help but admit that the meeting with this man had ruined my vacation. It would be the utmost of naiveté to take the count seriously. Yet he had, at his disposal, names, dates, facts. Why had I reacted so negatively to his assertions? I couldn't decide whether meeting him at the deserted beach had been a mere nuisance or a revelation. Upon cool reflection, I found it impossible to believe that he was Theodor, my old classmate. His improbable tale had the aura of insanity about it. On the other hand, why had he gone to all the trouble of pretending he was?

With these thoughts, I arrived in town. I went directly to the apartment, where I found a letter from my wife in the States, saying that our kids had finished school and camping and were about to leave, as planned, to join me in about two weeks.

I would go to Athens to meet them at the airport and then tour a few places, Olympia and Delphi among them, and return to the island, where we would stay at the apartment I had rented for the rest of our vacation. They all had met my father and Sophia in the States the year before.

Aristos, the cousin from whom I rented the apartment, had replenished the refrigerator, so I didn't have to go out for lunch in the heat of the day. I sliced a tomato and a cucumber and made a sandwich, adding salami and cheese. I drank a bottle of cold beer. The apricots were ripe, juicy, and as large as fists. I stuffed myself, and then, finding the apartment hot, I fell on the bed and remained torpid for several hours.

When I finally got up, it was only five thirty, and the afternoon was not getting any cooler. I looked outside. The deserted street was in flames. But my boredom exceeded my inertia, and I decided to step out.

I headed for the Marina, a part of the bayfront where I had seen a rent-a-car place as I was coming in three days ago. Broumis, a short, middle-aged fellow, snored on a chair, a *Playboy* magazine with an open centerfold on his knees, a fly swatter hanging from his hand. His jowls were sunken, and he hiccupped as he opened his eyes.

"Do you rent cars?" I asked in English, remembering the count's comment that I was flashing information a mile in advance.

"Yap," he responded in the same language and took me outside to a narrow yard at the back of his establishment, where two or three destroyed cars were parked under the sun. One was a black Lancia, whitened by half an inch of dust on its coat of paint; the other was a hearse-like Corina; and the third was a small, faded-red Fiat that looked like a getaway vehicle in a mobster movie.

The Fiat was the one I selected, and I followed the man inside to sign his papers. I gave him a twenty-dollar bill, and I charged the rest to my American Express card.

"Throw in the fifth once in a while to rest the motor," he advised me in his surly way, as if he were entrusting a treasure to my hands.

The Fiat had more zip to it than I had expected. It picked up nicely, though I gave myself a warning that I shouldn't jam on the brakes. I drove leisurely along the east coast, the part of the island that was getting shady this time of late afternoon. I had asked about Stephan before I came and was told about him by one of his cousins, a lady called Sotiria, whose house was only five or six kilometers from town and rather easy to find. It was a cool spot, freshened by the long shadows of the mountain and the sea breeze. A good-sized yard before Sotiria's house was planted with peach and pear trees.

I found Sotiria, her daughters, and her husband, Giorgos, all sitting on the veranda over the water, taking refreshments. They looked surprised to see me, but they knew who I was. We were neighbors before I left for America, and Sotiria and Marissa, my wife, who had lived on the island for a while, had been good friends.

"Bring a chair, Giorgos," Sotiria said to her husband, while she ran inside to get me a cup of coffee.

"What class were you in high school?" I asked Giorgos, a middle-aged man with heavy eyebrows, as soon as I sat down on the chair he brought me. Though I must have known him as a boy, I couldn't remember his face at all.

"You were in the same class with Stephan," said Giorgos. "I was two grades down."

"You and Stephan look alike."

"Lots of people think that."

"What is he doing now?"

"He's a lawyer, practicing in Athens. He's recently become the president of the Greek Lawyers' Association."

For some reason, I didn't like that turn of the conversation. It sounded like bragging.

Sotiria came in with a smile and a tray of fresh fruit, coffee, and cakes. She was so obliging and friendly that I decided to stay for a while, despite my growing dislike of Giorgos. I ate some of the fruit I was offered, sipped coffee from the demitasse cup, and enjoyed the view of the gulf and the clear, sharp mountain lines of Acarnania, only a few miles across the canal.

Sotiria's girls were in their bathing attire and soon trotted down to the beach for some late-afternoon sun. It was cool in the shade, but I felt restless.

"I have to go," I said, getting up.

"Why, you just came," Sotiria said, looking disappointed.

"I have to visit my father," I said, finding the best excuse I could.

"I have only seen him once since I arrived, and he must think I'm ignoring him."

"I was hoping you could stay the night," Sotiria said, not insisting.

I promised to come back and stay at least one night soon, maybe tomorrow night.

It was true I wanted to see my father, but when I got to town, it was evening, and I felt a little depressed and tired, so I went to the apartment. I could have stayed at Sotiria's, only I didn't like her husband, for some reason. In any case, as I felt rather sleepy, I took another snack from the refrigerator and went to bed.

In the morning, I decided to make true my intention and went to see my old father, whom I had seen only briefly since my arrival on the island.

I found him sitting in his yard, in the shade under his trellised vine, with its dusty, unripe grapes. He was writing something in his notebook, probably one of his poems. He was happy and a little surprised to see me, and he got up to give me a chair. His wife came out of the house, holding a tray with refreshments. She was also pleasant, as usual, and inquired about my vacation. I munched a roll or two—she baked excellent spiced ones—drank the coffee she brought me, and chatted with my father for a few minutes, asking about the progress of his poetry.

In his old age, he had started composing verses, and now some local literati had "discovered" him. They thought that his poems were a good example of "folk poetry" and had collected them into a volume, to be published soon. My father told me he was flattered, and, though he never presented himself as a poet, every time a guest was in the house, he read a poem or two aloud to him. He read to me his recent one, "Psipsina" ("The Kitten"); it detailed the kindness of animals, as contrasted to the callousness of humans.

"That colleague of yours came by yesterday afternoon," he said a few minutes later, as I was still eating some of my stepmother's cookies.

"Which colleague of mine?" I asked unsuspectingly.

"He said you were colleagues in the States. His name is Theodor, and he has a funny nickname—Vilmas or something."

"Theodor—what Theodor?" I said, stung.

"Well, actually, I'm supposed to know him, though I didn't recognize him. He said he is your godmother Olga's nephew. But it's been so long; I could hardly tell who he was at first."

"But did you actually recognize him? Is he really Theodor, Father?"

"I wasn't sure at first. But after he told me who he was, of course I recognized him."

"I mean, did you recognize him before he told you who he was?"

"No, how could I? It's been so many years. He lived with your godmother during the war. Then he went away—the Italians arrested him—and everyone said he was blown up in a minefield. But, as it happens, he survived. I'm glad to hear he's a university professor now."

"Who said he was?"

"He told me. He said you and he were together in Chicago and that he's followed your career closely. He spoke with great admiration about you. He thinks you're a first-rate scholar and teacher. You two must be great friends. He said that he'll settle that little monetary matter in a couple of days."

"What little monetary matter?"

"The money I let him have. He said this was an understanding between you two."

"Father, did you give him money?" I almost screamed.

"I said I did. I thought he was your friend. He said the banks were closed in the afternoon hours and that he couldn't cash his American Express checks. He'll return the money directly to you."

"How much did you give him?"

"Twenty-five thousand drachmas. Is there any problem?"

That was almost two hundred dollars. I felt sick, knowing that the money would never see my pocketbook again. I took out my wallet, drew out five five-thousand-drachma bills (I had been to the bank before I came), and handed them to my father.

"Here, Father," I said. "And, please, if a stranger comes to you quoting my name, don't give him money."

"But isn't he your godmother's nephew?"

"What if he is? I don't know. And I've never seen the man in the States."

"I can't take this money, then."

"Don't worry, Father. I'll see the man. He's in town."

I left him, keeping the rest of my thoughts to myself.

CHAPTER 27

The Visit

I went back to the apartment, depressed. After that conversation with my father, I didn't want to go anywhere or see anyone. I had been careless, as I hadn't paid sufficient attention to meeting this eccentric at Ai-Yiannis, thinking it was some kind of freak occurrence. I couldn't blame my father for being taken advantage of; besides, there would be nothing but embarrassment and waste of time if I tried to track down the impostor and deliver him to the police. I was worn out, so I let things be.

I decided to go to the beach for a swim, and since I had the means of transportation, it was easy. The strip of sand beach at the edge of town was crowded and hot, but the water was nice and cool, so I stayed in for a while. I knew nobody, and that suited me just fine. So far, I had at least achieved one thing: anonymity. I knew that as soon as I strolled around town with my father at my side, people would recognize me and join us. I avoided sitting at the café next to the sand beach, where a motley crowd gathered under a thatched roof, enjoying the breeze and large plates of spaghetti and meatballs. Frustrated by my experience, and still feeling lonesome, I drove back to the apartment, where I ate the rest of the stale food from that refrigerator. After a beer, I lay down on the bed and slept for a couple of hours, repeating yesterday's routine.

In the afternoon, I visited my father, who chatted with me for a couple of hours, regaling me with stories of his army days. He asked me if I'd seen the man to whom he'd given the money, and I said not yet, but I told him not to worry, that the matter would be settled. My stepmother, seeing I was half starved, prepared a nice dinner of broiled fish, soup, salad, desserts, and coffee, and I really felt good after that nutritious meal.

To pass the evening, I decided to go to the movies. I remembered from the old days the open-air theater, located a few blocks from the town square, with its rows of chairs in an enclosure between buildings, facing a wide screen on a wall.

I didn't find the old theater and was told by a white-haired man who ran one of the bookstands (nobody I recognized) that the establishment had moved down a few blocks, nearer to the Marina. This was where the big crowds gathered. I proceeded in that direction, shoving against the tide of a large throng that came in ceaseless waves. People sat at outdoor cafés, crowding the sidewalks, eating, chattering, tormented by noisy loudspeakers suspended overhead.

Finally, I found the theater. Its entrance was a narrow alley squeezed between tall buildings. I might have missed it, had it not been for a paper billboard, set up on a tripod in front of a tiny booth, announcing an old American western featuring John Wayne and Randolph Scott. I had seen that a long time ago in the States. No matter. It would be better than walking around.

I went up to the window to buy a ticket and was greeted by a fellow whose face looked familiar. He stared at me strangely too. But I couldn't place him. He was a handsome man of forty-five or so, youthful enough, but with completely white, close-cropped hair. He gave me the ticket and the change and said, "Thank you."

I said nothing else and was starting for the gate when a voice from behind me stopped me.

"Philios!"

I turned.

The man had come out of the booth and was approaching me with open arms. "Philios! Is it you?"

I instantly recognized him. "Panos!"

It was an emotional moment. This was indeed Panos, my boyhood friend, a man whose face I should never have forgotten. But time had dimmed my memory of his features; besides, he looked almost white. He left the ticket booth to a pretty woman, also with silvery-white hair. He took me to his office, housed in a small building next to the theater, and there, we both sat down and looked at each other. He ordered refreshments from a nearby café, and in a few minutes, a waiter came with lemonades and a slice of chocolate cake.

"Is this your place?"

"It's a summer job," he explained. "My father left me this lot, and we decided to operate a business on it during the tourist season. We of course reside in Athens. I am running a chain of open-air theaters in the suburbs. But Eleni and the girls like Ionia during the hot months, so we spend the summers here."

"Eleni?"

"Yes, my wife. You remember her. She is your cousin. You and I were in the same grade with her."

"I remember her very well. But she wasn't the lady who replaced you at the booth window?"

"Exactly. That was her."

"I had no idea. I thought she was one of your employees. She must think I was rude to her for not saying hello."

"Don't worry. I'm sure she didn't recognize you."

"How have you been?" I said, sipping the lemonade and eating the cake slowly. It was a sultry evening, but the breeze came through the window, and the cool revived my spirits.

"As I said, I run a good business. When my father died, I rented out his leather shop and moved to Athens. But the high tourist season brings a lot of people to the island these days, and it's likely to increase. I am thinking of starting a restaurant and maybe a hotel on the western beaches. Just for the summer, you understand. Eh, say, I heard your Greek-American wife is coming soon."

"How do you know that?"

"Oh, Sotiria is the center of news in town. We are related. Her husband's brother is married to my cousin Dina. You remember Stephan, don't you?"

"Indeed, I do. I heard he's a lawyer."

"And a big man too. He always was big, even when we were boys. He almost fought the war all by himself. He was in the army, where he gained distinction, before he became a lawyer."

I seemed ignorant of Stephan's military exploits.

"You know," said Panos, eager to fill in the missing details, "Stephan enlisted in the revolutionary army, fought in the guerilla force, and was wounded and decorated. Then he joined the regulars, went to Korea, and was wounded and decorated twice. On returning to civilian life, he entered the university and got his law degree. He practiced on the island, then ran as a deputy, won a seat in parliament, and then went back to law practice. He's done a lot. I wonder how a human being can do so many things. Eh, I heard you're doing pretty well yourself."

I modestly listed some of my accomplishments, not stressing anything in particular.

"Come on," he said. "Let me introduce you to Eleni."

That was a funny way of putting it, but after all, it had been more than twenty-five years since I had last seen her, and both of us were different persons. I followed him outside.

The lady was still sitting at the window, cutting tickets for some parties that were going in. The show was about to begin.

"This is Philios," Panos said to her, as soon as the parties were gone.

"Hello, Philios," she said, extending her hand nonchalantly from inside the booth. "I heard you were in town."

"How are you, Eleni?" I said with an equal degree of apathy.

So she knew who I was when I went in. She must have guessed, since she knew I had arrived. And I had tried so hard to remain in hiding.

New patrons were just arriving, so I stepped aside for a minute or two.

"Where are you staying?" Panos asked. I told him. "You must come and stay with us," he insisted. "We can't let you stay at an efficiency apartment, for heaven's sake!"

"You must," Eleni echoed from inside the booth. Then, since the customers were all in and the show had started, she came out and stood by us. I was stunned by her good looks. Despite her silver-white (no doubt dyed that color) close-cropped hair, her face was youthful, and she was as pretty as ever. She hardly looked more than twenty-five or thirty years old. I tried to count her years, certain she couldn't be younger than forty-four—same age as me and a year younger than Panos. She stood by Panos, and they were extremely well matched. A handsome couple. *Fate must have willed it; they deserve each other*, I said to myself, satisfied to see them looking happy together.

"You must come," she repeated. "Panos's house is only our summer home here, and the girls take up a lot of space, but we have a nice unoccupied guest room at the back. It's just right for a bachelor," she continued—and she saw I was blushing. "I mean, for someone staying alone for a while."

I knew what she meant. I said I would be glad to accept their polite offer and went inside to see the show, since more patrons had arrived and both of them looked busy issuing tickets.

When I came out, only Panos was there, and he repeated the offer. I said I would stay with them but didn't specify when. He shook my hand warmly, and then he hugged me. For just a second or two, I felt the warmth in my heart for my old, dear friend. But this feeling lasted only a few seconds.

I spent the better part of next day with my father, going around town with him, visiting my elderly relatives. Many were still alive and seemed happy and proud to see me. I enjoyed my visit with Aunt Vasiliki, my mother's sister. She was full of energy, as she had always been, and talkative. She brought back memories of my mother, for she looked like her. When I burst into tears, she scolded me, "Now you cry, but a letter or Christmas card from you I never had!"

It was true; I never had written to my relatives and hardly ever to my father. She let me take several pictures of her in her local costume with a camera I carried slung around my shoulder.

On our way back to the house, my father insisted we take a stroll in the Agora, the main street, where I could greet his friends. We were stopped several times by various individuals—who now recognized me when they saw me by his side, once outside the Church of Agios Menas—for a lengthy treatise by an acquaintance of his, who insisted I knew his son in high school. Of course, I had no recollection whatsoever of who he talked about.

"Let's say hello to Andrew," my father said, stopping before a baker's shop next to a colonnade that supported a new apartment complex.

"Andrew?"

"He lived in our house, remember?"

"Oh, that Andrew."

We entered the shop, where a little man wearing an apron stood behind a counter, handing loaves to costumers. He looked to be in his late sixties. He had a few tufts of hair left and flashed a broad, toothless smile.

"This is Philios," my father said.

"Philios?" The little man dashed forward from behind his counter and took my hand. "How are you, Philios? Your dad told me you were coming."

"I'm well," I responded. "And how are *you*?"

"Great, great."

"How's business?"

"Couldn't be better. I own the bakery now, all by myself."

"Do you have children?"

"Children, grandchildren, everything."

"Do you remember the Italians? The wedding party?"

"Oh, the party," he repeated, lost for a moment. "Yes, yes. Wasn't that wonderful?"

He kept shaking my hand, long after I had lost any interest in him. He and my father repeated a few jokes about how things were during the Occupation, and Andrew kept laughing. He must not have had enough ready cash—even in his current affluence, it seemed—to buy himself a set of teeth.

"Say hello to your wife," I said.

"Oh, there she is, outside, with two of our kids."

I noticed a woman sitting on one of the next-door café chairs, keeping an eye on a young boy and a girl, ages ten to eleven, who were running around the tables and playing. She looked fiftyish and had streaks of gray hair. She wore a faded designer dress with a pretense of elegance.

"That's Aspasia. You remember her? Go outside and say hello."

I did as he said but my father stayed inside to chat with his friend.

When I approached her table, the woman looked at me, a little puzzled, I thought.

"Are you ..." she mumbled. "Your father said you were coming."

"Yes," I said. "I am Philios. It's been a long time. How are you?"

"As you see," she said—sounding bitter, I thought. "Andrew and I have three children. The two you see here and Dionysius, who is studying at the University of Athens. He had straight A's in high school, and he went there on a scholarship. He just married last year and has a little baby girl. His ambition is to go to America one day to continue his studies there. Sit down; I'll order a Coke."

I sat at a table next to her. "That's outstanding," I said, pleased with the news. "But what's the matter with Andrew? He looks a bit thin to me."

"He's been like that since his mother and one of his sisters died in a car accident a few years ago. That shook him up for good. Besides, his business is down these days. Who can make money as a baker?"

"He was doing so well back then ... really good."

"Yeah, they all did well during the war. Thanasis ..." she mumbled, saving me a question about him I was going to ask, "was rich then too. But when the war ended and he returned to his butcher shop, he couldn't stand it. He started drinking, got bloated, was depressed, took pills, and one day, he dropped dead of a heart attack."

"Too bad," I said, without feeling anything. "And what about Adrianna?" I was not sure I should have asked.

"Ah, she was the smart one. She had gold coins for a dowry. That's why this Karandonis fellow married her. But she kept it from him—at least, most of it. And after one year, she left him, went to Athens, and started an affair with a guy. After a divorce, she married him. With her money, they opened a business, importing foreign goods or something, and she lives like a queen. She has three children too. She ended up being the lucky one."

Though my interests had altogether faded since I'd first known these women, I couldn't help but shiver, and I felt sweat dripping down my back. The past can be haunting, and Adrianna had been the woman who introduced me to the secrets of love.

As my father exited the bakery, I said a hasty goodbye to Aspasia and followed him home. My stepmother had prepared a nice lunch, and I drank some red wine, which made me woozy. I took a nap on a sofa in their tiny living room and awoke late in the afternoon. After my stepmother brought me coffee, I thought it was a good time to drive over to Sotiria's at the beach and clear my head of some tangled questions I had accumulated during my first few days of my return so far.

When I arrived, I sat on their balcony, and Sotiria brought me coffee and a bowl of fruit. Several other people were there, but they had gone down to the beach for a swim, including her husband.

"How is it going so far?" she asked me.

"Well, I did see an old friend."

"Panos?"

"How do you know about it?"

"He and his wife were here last night after the show. They are relatives of mine. I understand you were schoolmates with both him and his wife."

"Yes. His wife is my cousin."

"So how did you feel about seeing them again?"

"I felt they look fine together. A nice couple. Of course, they're different from the people I knew. They're not what my memory had retained of them."

"People change, you know. You grew up, and so did they, and you and Panos moved in two different directions."

"It appears lots of people did," I said vaguely.

"They're very nice. And Panos thinks very highly of you. University professor!"

I took this as a compliment, thanked her, and remained silent. I didn't want anyone to feel I was criticizing anybody.

The evening had advanced—it was almost dark—and most of the guests had returned from the beach and were sitting around the veranda, taking refreshments. Panos and Eleni and their two daughters had come too, and so had Stephan's wife, Dina, a woman in her forties, tall and dignified, with lots of pearls around her neck. Sotiria's girls also had brought with them a couple of other girls and two boys. Giorgos was there, eating from a bowl of fruit. This was too large a company to handle, and Sotiria was working overtime to bring refreshments to all of them. Fortunately, the young people, including Eleni's daughters, soon left for a nearby disco.

Sotiria brought me a tray on which there was a plate of lamb chops and cheese, salad, and watermelon. There also was wine and beer. I ate, despite the lateness of the hour and my fear that I was developing a bulging waistline while on vacation.

"And why hasn't Stephan come back yet?" Panos was asking.

"He had to go to a lawyers' convention at Salonika," Dina declared. "And he just came back from Paris. Then he has to stay in Athens for a week for another conference he will have to chair, and then he is scheduled to come to Ionia the second part of August, to catch the Fine Arts Festival."

"Busy man," Panos commented. "Not like the rest of us."

"Oh, you keep pretty busy yourself," Sotiria said, cutting him short. "Working hard in the summer as well as in the winter. Money-maker and soon-to-be Onassis."

"That's nothing." Panos tried to sound modest. "This is hardly doing anything. Just selling tickets to a crowd."

"You may think it's nothing, darling," Eleni cut in, with a slight testiness in her voice, "but keep in mind that we're managing a place. And that takes responsibility."

"That's right," Sotiria said. "You two need a vacation. Close the show down and take off and go to Corfu or somewhere for a week or two. I'll watch your daughters."

"No way," Panos said resolutely. "Business requires revenue. If we don't make money in the summer, how am I going to pay all those mortgages for the Athens theaters?"

"I'm sure we can make it," Eleni said, her fine eyebrows knitting into a frown. "We have more summer revenue than we'll ever need. But he wants to reinvest, and that's the problem. As soon as something is paid off, he starts a new schedule of payments."

This sounded like a family squabble, and I didn't want to hear the rest of it.

"Are you planning to go to the count's lecture?" Dina asked me after a moment or two. "It's only a few nights away."

"What count's lecture?" I asked, though feeling pretty certain I knew what she was talking about.

"A friend of her husband's, a professor or lecturer, is speaking about radioactivity harming us—or something like that," Sotiria hastened to inform me. "If you want my opinion, stay away. He says he's a poet or something like that. Last time he was here, everybody laughed at him."

"I beg your pardon," Dina proclaimed. "Stephan thinks highly of him. The count has studied physics, neurology, and the occult sciences. And he has published tons of verse. Of course, it's surrealistic or modernistic—nobody understands it—but he's a respected man in his circle. It's worth going to hear him, despite his obscure subjects. That's the whole point."

I noticed Dina's words commanded respect. Maybe that was because she was the wife of the mighty yet absent Stephan.

"I met this man," I said, "while I was at Ai-Yiannis a few days ago. He said he is a count. Do counts exist today?"

"That's one way of putting it," Dina responded. "When the Venetians occupied the Ionian Islands for centuries, they conferred the title *conte* to some favorite wealthy locals, mainly to help them collect taxes and to maintain the peace. One of my father's distant uncles called himself *Conte de Dioniso*. He was tall, still handsome in his fifties, and was known for his western dress, his fine horses, and his wit. He composed verses too."

"I've heard of such stories too," I said. "But this person I met is just a crude, pretentious wretch who claims he has known me since we were in high school. And he said he had followed my career in the States. I don't remember having ever seen him."

"But we did know him, Philios," Panos broke in. "He was organizing a group during the war, and we had agreed to undertake a certain mission together. It fell through because someone from our side squealed to the Italians. The count, as he now calls himself—he may be a count, for all I know—was arrested, tried, and sent to the execution squad."

"My father says the Theodor of those days was blown up in a minefield. And my father did not remember him, though he saw him a day or two ago. I mean, he saw him and didn't recognize him until the count told him who he was." I did not mention anything about his borrowing money from my father because I did not want to get deeper into this dispute.

"But it's been so long," Panos insisted. "People change in appearance, even in personality."

"Nevertheless," I countered, "I didn't believe anything he said."

"So you aren't going to hear him?" Dina asked.

"I didn't say I will or won't. I may go, just to spend an idle hour."

I had the impression my answer didn't quite meet the company's expectations because there was silence for the next few minutes. I was getting ready to go when Sotiria took me aside and asked me to stay there for the night. I said no, as I had to be busy fixing the apartment because my family would be here soon.

When I got up to go, I received disappointed stares from both Panos and Eleni and a frozen nod from Dina, who was also spending the night there. I was oppressed to hear their support for the impostor, who, by now, had spoiled my return home. If that man was Theodor—at this point, a possibility—I would feel awkward for the rest of my trip.

CHAPTER 28

The Dinner

The next morning, I visited my father, and we chatted for a while, and I let him read his poems. The man who had "discovered" him and was now making selections of his poems to publish in a book came in, and we had a brief talk about their literary value. He was middle-aged and pleasant, but I didn't want to get into a longer discussion, for fear of offending my father. Besides, I was pleased to see my father recognized. I excused myself, saying I had to get the apartment ready, as my family was coming soon. I asked the owner of the apartment if he could get us some extra plates, kitchenware, and other items needed for the coming visit of several persons.

Early that evening, I went to see Panos. I felt that my behavior to him and his wife last night might have been tactless. Maybe they found my entire attitude distant or aloof. The truth was, both of them had tried hard to impress me with their wealth and status, and I hadn't been impressed enough. Something in their efforts to renew our relationship seemed strained, despite mutual good intentions. *Was it my fault?* I wondered.

Panos was pleased to see me. He was busy working on his schedules for the evening shows at nine and eleven, he explained. He was showing two different movies, the late one being advertised as "adult."

He said that after the first show, he and his family would be having dinner at a new restaurant that was a couple of kilometers from town. He added that he and Eleni would be happy if I joined them.

I was eager to put them at ease, so I accepted. I stayed on until the first movie was over; then we drove to his house together in his blue BMW, a car in good condition but at least ten years old. His house was the same one I'd known, in the old neighborhood where I had grown up. I felt a pang as soon as I walked up the familiar old lane, and childhood memories crowded my mind. My father's old house (which my father had sold after the 1948 earthquake), just next to Panos's, had changed; the balcony had disappeared, and a large veranda had been added. The yard also had been built on, and the whole structure had lost its old flavor.

Panos's house looked exactly as before on the outside, but the inside had been modernized. There was bright wallpaper in the living room and the furniture was upbeat, with a color TV and a stereo and large woofer in the corner. Music was playing, and the two girls were dancing to a tune I only vaguely recognized as a type of rock. The girls resembled each other so much that they could have been twins, but Panos had said they were a year apart. The older, Lina, was nineteen and preparing to enter law school in Salonica—Uncle Stephan had given a helping hand during her preparation. The younger girl, Penelope, had no college ambitions for the moment; she wanted to become a singer or model. Both wore tight shorts and had spiked hairdos—out of place, even in a town with scores of weird-looking visitors.

The two girls nodded nonchalantly to me and rushed off to get dressed. Eleni came out, uttering an "Ah!" of surprise when she saw me, very unlike the apathetic *hello* my presence had evoked a few nights ago. She looked fabulous in a strapless white dress that matched her hair and contrasted her beautiful black eyes.

Panos went upstairs to get dressed, and we were left alone for a few minutes.

"I gather you don't like the count," she said, picking up a topic that had caused some consternation among her group the other night.

"He said he knew me, both here and in the States—quite well, in fact. I don't see how this can be true. I do not remember him at all."

"Why is that unusual?"

"It is to me. I remember having known people or people having known me. Had he been in the places he claims, I would not have forgotten that. Have you ever seen him?"

"I know absolutely nothing about the man, except that one of my relatives is raving about him, while another thinks him crazy."

"Did you go to college, Eleni?" I said, using her name for the first time. It was a soft, lulling sound that brought back, in a flash, a memory of her praying in her nightdress, long, long ago.

"No, I didn't. My father didn't even let me finish high school. You do remember that."

"Sorry, but I don't." It was true that I had forgotten much about her—as well as many other things—after I left Ionia at seventeen to go to Athens to prepare for my college entrance to America.

"Well, about that time, I was seventeen, and Panos was a year older. He persuaded his father to go to my father and ask for my hand. Then, things got really tangled. My father had heard about my liaison with Panos and took me back home to the village. But Panos's father had money. His business was thriving, and his investments abroad, not affected much by the war, made him a rich man. So, not only did my father not have to give me a dowry but he was extended credit to pay for his debts, as the war had ruined him."

"How about your sisters?"

"They didn't finish school, of course, other than grade school, but Panos used some connections to get them jobs in Athens. They're both married now."

"I'm glad things worked out for you and Panos," I said rather indifferently.

"Money does things," she said—a bit sarcastically, I thought. "Imagine—both our parents were so embarrassed by our young ages that they didn't want to announce our marriage, so we ended up going to a monastery and getting married by monks!"

Instantly, Panos's bubbled-headed idea to elope and find a monk to marry him and Eleni came back to mind. "After all, he got his wish," I said. "Congratulations to both. You seem a happy couple."

"That's my story. How about you?"

Panos came down, dressed in a striped shirt and light jacket, so I didn't have time to give an answer. I noticed the gold chain around his neck. He was tall and handsome with his silver hair, and I again was amazed at how perfectly matched they looked.

The girls came down too, in sport shirts and jeans, looking as casual as many of their American counterparts. They hardly said a word to me all evening; I guessed that was because I hadn't been sufficiently impressed by their sexiness.

The Garden Tavern was a cool spot, hidden under trellised vines and wide-leaved mulberry trees, with enough openings to let the breeze through. Three or four musicians were tuning up their instruments, and a man toted a bassoon, which offered an ox-like note here and there.

The food was tasty and well served. Panos had ordered lamb cooked in small spits, broiled flatfish from the fish farms, and fried eggplant in a succulent meat sauce. There was red wine and dark German beer. We all ate heartily for a while. The girls drank soft drinks, Eleni just sipped wine, and Panos consumed a great deal of beer. Eleni's eyes were riveted on me, and I tried not to stare back. Though her daughters were both good-looking, she far surpassed them. I controlled my drinking so that I could keep my stares within the bounds of propriety. There was no question of Panos's being jealous; he was getting too drunk for that. The girls' attention was soon drawn by the dancers on the floor. After half an hour or so, the music turned upbeat, the lights dimmed, and the dancing crowd became thicker; the girls were absorbed into it. Panos drawled incoherent words and leaned back in his chair, as if about to fall asleep.

I called for the bill, but Panos, suddenly revived, grabbed me by the arm, took a stack of banknotes from his pocket, and paid the waiter, leaving a large tip. When we got to the car, it was obvious he was in no condition to hold the steering wheel. I took over and drove the stick shift, barely managing to get out of the crowded lot. The area had been so overbuilt that I could hardly recognize the streets at night, but Eleni directed me, and we arrived at their house safely. The girls had stayed behind.

"There is no sense in your going back to that apartment at this hour," Eleni protested, as I was about to leave. "Besides, we have the guest room out there doing nothing. Stay for the night."

"S-sh-tay!" Panos drawled. "We will-l-l … t-t-take care of you."

I couldn't decline an offer so politely made. Besides, I was tired and wanted nothing but a bed to lie on. Eleni took me to the back of the house, where an addition had been built. It was a good-sized room, with a private bath, and a closet full of cotton towels, sheets, and beach items.

"But I don't have anything with me," I protested again. "I haven't come prepared to be a guest."

"There's most of what you need in these drawers," she said, pointing to a chest against the wall. "You can find shaving materials in there." She pointed to the bathroom. "Make yourself at home."

She left me; I was dazed and sleepy. I fell on the bed as I was and slept uneasily, as I do every time I eat late and too much.

In the morning, when I got up, Panos was already gone, and Eleni's girls were taking their time in bed, having stayed out till late. Eleni gave me a breakfast of boiled eggs, rolls, and American cereal, which she said she had brought from Athens, but no one ate it. Her daughters usually breakfasted and lunched out, and her husband only drank coffee till noon. Then he had a heavy lunch and napped till four or five in the afternoon.

I politely thanked her for the breakfast and got ready to take my leave.

"Tonight is the count's lecture," she reminded me as I was about to step out the door, "and no doubt you will be there. Come back here when it's over. The house is only a few blocks, and your room will be waiting."

"Where is the lecture?" I asked, stopping for a moment.

"Why, of course at our theater. The count rented it from Panos, who would not refuse an old friend a favor!"

That was useful information to keep in mind. I walked away from her house, feeling worn out by my fruitless attempts to renew old friendships. This morning, I had experienced a vague loathing for the drunk Panos and annoyance at his wife's no-so-subtle attempts to allure me. At least, that is how I interpreted her invitation to go back.

I renewed the car rental at Broumis's, and when that job was finished, I walked around town, photographing old wooden houses not yet swept away by the modern mania to build square cement boxes, with bare flat roofs baked by the sun.

I also visited the gift shops along the bay and bought cards and small gifts for my friends back home. I was a little shocked to see posters all over the place announcing the count's lecture that night. It wasn't until that moment that I thought of this event as an actual possibility. Would people really pay to listen to this bizarre individual?

Then I visited my father and had lunch with him and his wife. Afterward, I slept through the afternoon at the rented apartment. For some reason, I paid extra attention to my attire as I went out for the evening. I had no second thoughts or reservations. I went straight to Panos's theater, intending to ferret out some information about Theodor from him, though not exactly knowing what. I found Panos busy with his books again. He seemed genuinely pleased to see me and ordered refreshments from the nearby café.

"I must say I'm embarrassed about last night," he said apologetically. "I don't often drink—or drink that much. It's only that I'm exhausted by this damned rut I'm in, working throughout the summer, just to keep things rolling. You don't know the responsibilities that I've amassed."

I made no comment, and he continued venting his frustrations and detailing his problems. All I understood was that he had driven himself into a financial impasse and that he was trying to recover. He explained that he was suffering from *anchos*, an anxiety disorder—a modern form of being haunted by real or imaginary fears. At the same time, he assured me that he still had assets—his father had left him considerable property, as yet untouched, and he had no fear of financial failure.

He talked for half an hour or so, during which time my mind often strayed. I had begun to make certain conjectures of my own.

"Tell me one thing, Panos," I said, after he had just about exhausted his topic. "You are renting your theater tonight to this … count."

"Yes," he said, straining for an answer. "He is a friend, and I'm doing this for a friend, not really for business reasons. But he insisted we go fifty-fifty of the gate."

"But are you really sure this man is Theodor, the schoolmate we both knew back then, during the war? Are you absolutely sure?"

Panos looked both annoyed and thoughtful for a moment, and he didn't reply right away. "To tell you the complete truth," he said, "I'm not really sure if he is. He has the same stocky build that Theodor had, and in that respect, he seems fine. But his voice, face, and every other personal detail suggest absolutely nothing. He could and he couldn't be Theodor."

"Then how can you rent him the theater? Don't you fear that he could be an impostor who's deceiving both you and the rest of the town?"

"He came up with so many details about our plan to assassinate Massos. I figured nobody else could have known these things, except him, Stephan, you, and me. Those facts he cited have almost convinced me of his identity."

"He had facts with me too. He told me a lot of things I did in the States, facts that no one but me would have known. Still, that does not make him the true Theodor. A clever impostor could have gotten hold of those facts. But there is something else you must know. The other day, he went to my old father, pretending he and I know each other, that we are colleagues, and he borrowed money from him, saying he would return this money to me. I haven't seen that money. I haven't seen him."

"That's because he's at the beach, preparing for his lecture."

Panos seemed almost impervious to my logic. I wondered it was worth pursuing my topic with him.

"How did you get to know him? I mean, this man?"

"I met him through a connection. And when he told me who he was, I let him use the theater. He seemed to have talked here before; that is, before I started using this property." He took a bottle out of one of his drawers and two small glasses, offering me one.

I refused. "Did he ever say anything about me?"

"Not a word. Never mentioned your name. But the old Theodor did."

"How do you mean?" I asked.

"I received a letter from the early Theodor, soon after people heard he'd been blown up in a minefield. You must have heard that yourself."

"I don't remember. That must have been the time I spent at my grandfather's, after the Germans came in."

"Perhaps. In any case, in his letter, he wanted me to know he wasn't dead and that he was joining the guerilla forces to fight the Germans."

"Why didn't you let me know—later, when I came back to town—that you'd had a letter from him?"

Panos hesitated, gulping down another shot of whiskey before answering. "That letter mentioned you. He said you went to the prison to visit him before he was taken from the island, and that you stood under the wall, and that he knew then it was you who had passed the word to Massos." He poured me a drink.

I took a few sips before getting up to leave.

Panos gave me a pained look. "In the same letter, he told me that you were in love with Eleni too."

I took a few more sips, but I made no response.

He poured himself more. "And that she loved you. I don't know how he got hold of such ideas."

As he said those things, Panos no longer looked real. I thought he might be his double. *Funny thing*, I thought. *There are two Theodors, two Panoses, two Elenis. I too must have a double.*

Ionia too had leaped out of its former self and gained another identity. One was the old, war-torn, peaceful little island, forgotten by everyone except a few tired Italian and German soldiers. The other was the new—a gaudy, tourist-hungry, arrogant resort, apathetic and a bit decadent. No place for me to have come back to.

We did not say anything else. I waited until he was finished with his books (he had taken more whiskey sips by them—and I helped him with the bottle); then, we both drove to his place, where Eleni had prepared an appetizing supper. The girls were there with their boyfriends, and I had leisure to observe a Greek yuppie family at dinner. The girls talked about movies—*Rocky II, Saturday Night Fever*—as well as Cher and John Travolta. I sat through that adolescent gibberish, my only entertainment being my stealing glances at the hostess. I had to make efforts to keep my eyes off her forbidden face, thinking her husband might be jealous.

But Panos drank, oblivious of me, of her, of anything. He would have paid no attention if Godzilla had barged in and knocked the walls down.

CHAPTER 29

The Lecture

After dinner, I went out for a walk, mixing in with the crowds that had begun to gather in the streets, sit in the open-air cafés and restaurants, or endlessly stroll back and forth at the bayfront. It was a warm evening, but the breeze from the west started cooling things off.

I walked until about nine o'clock; then I drifted toward the open-air theater, still not having decided whether I would attend the count's lecture. I kept turning back, but then, impulsively, I turned in the direction of Panos's establishment. If nothing else, the lecture would give me a clue as to the questions that had been prevalent in my mind of late. Was the count a fraud or the man I once knew?

If he, as he said, indeed was Theodor, why didn't he confront me openly? Why had he taken money from my father? For revenge? In that case, could he not then threaten me in some way? It was worth the trouble of finding out. The question was, how could his lecture tell me anything?

When I arrived at the theater, a crowd was waiting outside in a line, not moving forward. Panos was not at the booth, but a man outside sat on a stool behind a small table, selling tickets. He had a bald spot, with graying hair left at the temples, and a black moustache, the ends of which hung over the sides of his lips.

"The gentleman?" he inquired, as if I had gone there for some unfathomable purpose.

"May I purchase a ticket?"

"Oh," he said, and he handed me an envelope with two tickets. "Compliments of the count."

"Thank you," I said, taking the tickets. "Why are these crowds waiting outside?"

"In five minutes"—he winked at me—"the price will be knocked down by 10 percent."

I did not accept the count's gift and paid him two hundred drachmas, about a dollar and a half. He smiled, seeing me going in. A few persons were already inside, all sitting in the front rows. I sat in a side seat, camouflaged under some wide tree leaves that were peeping over a wall from an adjoining backyard. There was a platform in front of the screen, partly covered with a backcloth, where the name and title of the count were awkwardly scrawled in large letters. On the platform, a podium had been installed, with a microphone on it. Just above the screen, on the side of one of the buildings that enclosed the theater arena, there was a balcony, on which several people were already gathered to watch the show. More balconies around were also getting crowded, as were the windows. I wondered what made these people want to listen to the phony lecture that I knew was coming. But then it occurred to me that I was there to listen to it myself. In my case, though, there was an ulterior motive.

I had no time for too much self-analysis. I heard a roar, and the crowd from outside rumbled in like a stream that had just broken a dam. The price of tickets had been lowered. People leaped over the seats to get a better view; they pushed and shoved and shouted at each other, or they called out to their company. There were parents with small children, young men and women, old folks, even two priests in their black robes and cassocks. An octogenarian who sat next to me had brought his worry beads, which he fingered with impatience. Some boys were holding Frisbees. Most of the customers were eating dried pumpkin seeds and chickpeas from paper cones as they talked idly to each other.

In about five minutes the arena was filled to capacity. Spectators hung from balconies above like clusters from a vine, and the windows were jammed. Again, I wondered what made all these crowds come to hear this man? Well, I was soon to find out.

Suddenly, a voice from an invisible announcer (who must have been in the projector room behind me) blared out of the loudspeakers suspended on both sides of the screen.

"Welcome to this distinguished event, ladies and gentlemen. Tonight, we are all honored to have with us a man whose presence makes the big cities shake with envy, a man famous at the universities both here and abroad. He is a poet whose magical words and prophetic strains will be harped throughout the world. Tonight, his topic is—let's hear a cheer—'Ingratitude Is Radioactivity'! A round of applause, ladies and gentlemen, for Count Theodor de Vilamontis!"

A roar rose from the crowd.

The count appeared on the platform. He was dressed exactly as I had seen him in the cave at Ai-Yiannis, with his long-sleeved shirt and bow tie. He waved stiffly at the crowd and then grabbed the microphone with resolution.

"Women and men!" he started, his voice settling to a falsetto baritone. "Sense does not allow me to call you 'ladies and gentlemen.' Those species of human beings are now extinct! There is no upper society; there are only upper minds!

"Hurray to upper minds!"

"Myself, I have pulverized in humility in order to serve you. Buddha, Mohammad, Saint Francis, Tolstoy, and Mahatma Gandhi embodied compassion. I'm a downtrodden wretch who fought and went to prison. Some of you walk around without seeing the luminous light of the stars! Don't you see the stars?"

His eyes turned skyward. His hand waved a handkerchief—as large as a tablecloth, with red squares on it—wiping the perspiration on his head. A firecracker burst.

"Yes, Count, we see the stars. What about them?"

"Dust there is on the stars, dust on earth, dust in your souls. The Great Spirit comes but once in centuries. I am the flames! You are the ashes! You are ungrateful to the masters. Ingratitude is radioactivity!"

"Don't burn yourself, Count. Then you'll turn into ashes too!" a voice boomed from the arena.

"I am what I am. A sword that cuts both ways. You are what you are. Blunt kitchen knives. Your existence manures the earth for the genuine plants to sprout. There is hope if you listen to the prophets. You have strewn the streets with rosebuds. Do it more often! You read poetry at your festivals. Do it again!"

Two flying saucers were hurled toward him but missed him. He ducked behind the podium but soon reemerged.

"And here comes the question that will incinerate your intestines! The black-robed devils who whisper in your ears—ban them!"

The audience roared.

"And the true masters are forever scoffed!" the count went on. "I secretly weep for you. I, for you all. Ingratitude is radio—"

He had no time to finish. A bucket full of dirty water, dropped from the balcony above him, splashed on his head, knocking him unconscious on the platform. The crowd howled, like demons loose from hell.

People stampeded toward the main exit. Two policemen climbed up the platform and administered first aid to the unconscious count. I looked for an escape. My way out ahead of me was blocked by the sea of the pushing and shoving mob.

Fortunately, I was sitting next to a side exit. I opened it and ran for my life. I walked back to Eleni's, drained of all feeling. I went there because I couldn't think of anywhere else to go at this late hour. I just wanted to get away from it all, go to bed, and fall asleep.

There was no answer when I knocked on the door. I thought that was strange because she had told me she would be at home tonight. I knew that Panos was to stay for the second show—the movie he was showing—if, indeed, any patrons chose to go into that madhouse to watch a motion picture.

I tapped on the door again, but no one seemed to be inside.

That was strange. Maybe I wasn't welcome. I knocked for the third time. Again, no answer. I had been standing before the door for five minutes now. I started walking away, intending to go back to my apartment, but then, instinctively, I pushed the door lightly. It was unlocked. Maybe Eleni was asleep and had forgotten to lock it. I pushed it open completely and saw a light in the living room, though no one was there. I knew my way, so I tiptoed to the guest room. I turned on a small lamp on the dresser next to the bed. The sheets were fresh, which meant I was expected. Well, there was no sense waiting around, so, fully dressed as I was, I turned off the light and lay down on the bed. I could hear the ticking of an alarm clock on the dresser and, vaguely, the sound of accordions coming from a tavern not far from the bayfront. Most bayfront restaurants had music going on all night. *Good*, I thought, *that will lull me to sleep.*

I must have dozed off, but I thought I heard a slight knock on the door.

A voice came in a whisper. "Philios?"

I got up and turned on the light. It was a tiny lamp, and the weak bulb gave only a faint light. I could hardly see who was at the door. In my half sleep, I hadn't recognized the voice. Maybe it was dream.

But it wasn't at all a dream. There, standing in the now- opened door, was Eleni, in her nightdress—of truly thin and transparent fabric, something made only for moments of guilt and lust.

I was still sitting on the bed and made as if to stand up.

"Don't!" she whispered, with a small movement of her beautiful wrist.

"What is it?" I said. "I have just come back from the count's lecture."

She did not seem to hear what I said but sat next to me on the bed. "I'm very unhappy," she said, and tears flooded her eyes. "I have wasted my life! Panos is a failure, and all my dreams with him have crashed."

I said nothing, unable to find the right words. I felt whatever I said would be indelicate.

"I was too young," she continued. "The rushed marriage prevented my even finishing high school. I had to help him run his business—first here and then in Athens. He said we were married and partners in everything. I became his secretary, his typist, his errand girl, and even my two pregnancies didn't stop me from slaving for him. Now, I am middle-aged, unwanted—I feel it—uneducated, and aimless for the rest of my life."

"Eleni, why are you telling me all this?"

"I thought you cared," she said and moved closer to me on the bed.

"I did, then," I said. "But people change, and you can't repeat the past."

The tiny wrinkles around her mouth lengthened, and I could tell her real age. But she was still ravishing.

"Panos loves you," I said. "And you two are raising a family. You will be fine." I leaned forward and gave her a soft kiss on the cheek. It was the first physical contact I'd had with the woman I had loved a long time ago.

With that, I got up, opened the door, and went on my way.

CHAPTER 30

Revelations

There was only one way for me to go—back to Panos's establishment. He was still in his booth, leaning back on his chair, a half-empty bottle of beer in his hand.

He got up when he saw me and started apologizing for what had happened in Theodor's show. "It was horrible," he said. "I never thought people in this town would behave like savages."

I cut him short and told him the reason I had come back. "I want to see Theodor," I said. "Do you know where he is staying?"

"Oh, sure," he said readily. "Just behind the projection booth, there is a tiny apartment. I sometimes use it to sleep in when I have more than one show and I'm too tired to go home. I let him have it for as long as he is in town. You'll find him there."

I walked there, found the little place—just a square box, really—and knocked on the door. After a few minutes, a sleepy and yawning Theodor, in a bathrobe, appeared at the door.

"Oh, it's you," he said. "Come in."

I stepped inside and saw that, despite its miniscule size, the place was well furnished—a nice bed, a chair or two, a small desk—a tiny kitchen, and a bathroom at the back.

"I was expecting you," he said, still yawning hideously. "Sit down."

I sat awkwardly in one of the chairs, which creaked a little.

"I know why you came," he said, stretching and sitting on the bed. His robe was a faded green, and he apparently had taken a shower, for his hair was still wet.

"Let me ask you a direct question," I said. "Are you or are you not the Theodor I knew then? Just tell me in a few words, and I'll leave you alone."

"But I've already told you who I am—who I was. Do you want me to take an oath?"

"Then I came to apologize for what I did to you, giving you up to the Italians and sending you to prison."

"Ah, that's all water under the bridge. You can forget it. And you are forgiven."

"Then why all the parade of stories you told me at Ai-Yiannis? How did you get hold of all those facts about my career in the States? And were you there yourself?"

"Those were tall tales," he said, still yawning.

"Yes, but how did you get hold of such facts?"

"You want a beer?"

"No."

"Wine?"

"No."

"Sprite?"

"For heaven's sake, no! Just answer my question!"

"How about whiskey?" he persisted, determined, it seemed, to drive me crazy, as he had done a few days ago at the beach.

But I said yes, just to get a response from him.

He pulled out a bottle that could have been on the shelves since antediluvian times, but whiskey ages well, so I took a couple of sips directly from the bottle.

"Listen," he said, as if waiting for me to get a bit tipsy (which I was getting), "I learned things about you from different sources, one of whom was a man called LaGoudas…."

"Basil LaGoudas?"

"Yes."

"How in the world did you find him?"

"He was giving a lecture at the Parnassus Club in Athens, and he mentioned your name. I approached him afterwards and told him you and I were in the Resistance and then he and I had coffee together and he told me most of the things you heard at the beach. Nice fellow, really...."

I was too stunned at this devil's coincidence to say anything.

"The truth is, I was never in the States," Theodor went on.

"How about all the other stuff you said, about you being at Berkeley, for instance?"

"Oh, I read these things at the newspapers, or made them up. I am a con man and was from the start. When I was kicked out of the Zervas units—they thought I was a Communist—I drifted from place to place, doing all kinds of odd jobs: brick-laying, road construction, boxer—always taking a fall for cash—hashish distributor in a pub in Piraeus, and what have you. That lasted until I met a man who said I could become a poet and an actor. He also said he was a surrealist. Big deal, he said. He took me under his wing, so to speak, and he and I went around small towns, put on shows, and let the audiences know that we were clowns. They expected a laugh, and we let things roll along. That was a con job, to be sure, but by this time, I didn't care. I got used to overripe tomatoes, rotten eggs, and other trash thrown in my face, not to mention dishwasher emptied on my head, but the cash rewards—well, let's say it was a living."

I took another sip from the bottle, and he took one too. We sat back and laughed, like two fellows in a puppet show.

"Eventually," he continued, "he and I parted ways, and then I went as a solo act. I 'studied' surrealism—they said it was in vogue—learned to recite nonsense verse, and pretended I was a poet and a count. The rest you know."

"How about your act at the beach? Why go through it?"

"Well, it was sort of a getting-back-at-you tactic. Fibs are rooted in human nature, and that one just fell in my lap. I knew you had gone there. As things stand, no harm done."

"And what about getting money from my old father?"

"Just rubbing it in. I can return the money."

"Forget it. But you and Panos? You were friends. Did he know all this?"

"Panos is a nice fellow, and for old times' sake, he let me use his theater. I think that he, like me, needed the cash. Business is no good in open-air theaters today. Besides, I had been here before, and the people knew me. My fake name as Count de Vilamontis became part of popular lore, and I was accorded the name 'Poet Laureate of Lunacy' by the townspeople. So Panos, who remembered me from the old times, accepted taking me in for a show, but his cut was fifty-fifty."

"Is his business in such bad shape?"

"Bad says nothing. His business in Athens is falling apart. People don't go to open-air theaters for movies anymore. They prefer discos, nightclubs, and late-night restaurants. And big TVs have wrecked the open-theater business. And Panos claims that his wife and daughters are ruining him. For his wife's sake, he rented a luxury apartment in an upscale neighborhood in Athens, and with that, he went over the limit. I'm not so sure he'll last much longer. He might go back to his father's business—leather. He still has assets. But that would require living in a small town—and that's a no-no to his wife."

I said nothing for a while and took the last sip from the whiskey bottle. I didn't want to wish him good luck (for what?), so I got up to go.

He took me to the door. "You were the best of the lot," he said, and I saw some moisture in his eyes.

"You're not a bad poet yourself," I said and went through the door.

I didn't want to stop to see Panos—he was still in the booth and getting ready to lock up the place, as the show was over—but he saw me.

"Eh," he said. "How goes it in there?"

"Oh, we just reminisced a bit. He is okay."

"Fine," he said. "Would you like to go back home with me? The guest room is available."

"No," I said. "I am leaving tomorrow morning. But we will be back in town with the family in a few weeks."

"Okay," he said, and he extended his hand.

"May I ask you a question, Panos?"

"Yes, of course," he said. "Shoot."

"Those two boys across the street from us? Nionios and Avantamos. What happened to them?"

Panos scratched his beard, stifling a yawn. "Nionios is still around, shoeing horses. But he lost his wife when she slipped and fell in the street. As for Avantamos, he finally finished high school and went into the army. He rose in the ranks, and he is a colonel today. He helped his sister to get an education, and she is now married and living in Athens. They said he is due to be promoted to brigadier general soon."

That exploded in my ears like a benign bomb. Some good news, finally!

I shook Panos's hand, and he went his way. A church bell chimed twice.

In the morning, I visited my father, who was up early and sipping his coffee. I explained to him that I was taking the bus to Athens, but I would be back with the family in a couple of weeks. He grouched a bit, saying he had hardly seen me, but I assured him I would be with him a lot more on the second visit.

I had delivered the car to Broumis the previous afternoon. Going by bus was the logical way to travel, I thought. A car meant driving in the heat, plus having an unreliable vehicle on roads I did not know well. Buses were not air-conditioned, but if I took the early one, I wouldn't suffer too much from the heat through the five or six hours of the ride to Athens.

As the bus turned north, scampering on the causeway that ran parallel to the reedy fences of the fish farm, I looked at the vistas of lagoons, sand strips, and beaches in the distance as I slowly took in what I had heard.

When the bus reached the end of the causeway, where it had to go over the bridge and cross to the mainland, I began to whistle a song, an old tune I had heard from a colleague when I was in the army. I sang the two lines I remembered out loud, though they weren't much:

> Open the door, Richard,
> Open the door and let me in!

It's this town, I said to myself, suppressing the bubble in my chest. I had just discovered I was still a part of the nuttiest place in the world. Still, my first love was there.

The bus, now on the other side of the bridge, gathered speed. I looked away into the horizon of shifting mountaintops until they all disappeared, one by one. I knew I had regained a part of my youth. Love has its ways. The reflection of Eleni's almond-shaped eyes reminded me that though you cannot repeat the past, you could not totally uproot it.

One more turn at the foot of Mount Lamia, and the waters changed hues. The blue deepened, and the wavelets sparkled as the sunlight grazed their tops.